About the Author

Kathy Viedge was born in South Africa and lived on a trading station in the Eastern Cape.

In the early 1960s, she moved to London. She was awarded a place at a drama school and trained to be an actress.

She returned to South Africa, where she taught at the University of Cape Town. She later joined a theatre company and has worked in the film industry. Kathy worked for a number of years as a producer in both radio and television.

She became interested in alternative therapy and returned to England to study Kinesiology and Reiki. She lives with her husband; they have two children, a son and a daughter.

Dedication

For my beloved family

Dedication

Acknowledgements

Kris for her enduring care and support.
Ingo and Antje who believed in me.
Carena for her help and invaluable insight.

Fifty years ago, I bought a typewriter and wrote a book inspired by the unique experience of the Swinging Sixties.

When 18-year-old Nina arrives in London she does not find the flower children, instead she meets people facing isolation, addiction and death. Young and alone they seek comfort from a large toy panda bear, the silent witness to their fractured lives.
It is also Nina's story, who in her struggle to find her own words learns to be happy.

The Peppermill, an almost forgotten manuscript, is an authentic voice of another time.

Kathy Viedge

THE PEPPERMILL

AUSTIN MACAULEY PUBLISHERS™

LONDON • CAMBRIDGE • NEW YORK • SHARJAH

A CIP catalogue record for this title is available from the British Library.

ISBN 9781528920292 (Paperback)
ISBN 9781528963046 (ePub e-book)

www.austinmacauley.com

First Published (2019)
Austin Macauley Publishers Ltd
25 Canada Square
Canary Wharf
London
E14 5LQ

Chapter One

When I was eighteen years old, all I wanted was a dark place like death. In the silence, I took comfort from the belief that what is hardest is best. I had to know I had courage; it was a requirement of my soul. I closed the door behind me, careful not to make a sound and walked away from yesterday.

I arrived at Waterloo Station, calmed by the large "Take Courage" posters along the railway line, believing it was a sign, not realising it was a beer. I had fled my parent's remote home in Ireland to secure my survival. Some years ago, my parents were involved in a near-fatal car crash. It had left my father with a shattered hip and a painful limp. My mother had suffered serious facial injuries, leaving her scarred and disfigured. My mother had insisted she needed to be able to watch the world go by now that she was no longer a part of it. Bitter and resentful, she would stand at the window and look down the hill at the closed-up houses where the people who remained grew old and died. I was incidental, except as a witness, to their distorted lives.

Unsure what to do after I left Waterloo Station, I walked through a small park with the names of dead people and bronzed angels. It was a funny afternoon, scruffy and overcast with a few people fluttering about. It was only after I left the park and had walked into the busy streets that I missed the scent of flowers.

It was disconcerting to be amongst so many people. I saw my reflection in a shop window. I was still dressed in the clothes bought from catalogues, a grey skirt with a white blouse and an old cardigan, sensible walking shoes, my long dark hair with its heavy fringe hanging over my face. I could not live as this thin shapeless person. There were lots of small shops that smelt sweet inside, a smell that would become very familiar, hash. It was the early sixties, the great sexual revolution had begun; I would at least dress the part. On Bond Street, I passed a small hairdressing salon and went in. They were not very busy. The girl who had shampooed my hair asked me what style I wanted. I had not thought of a style; I just wanted my hair cut. A thin wiry man who had glanced up at me when I came in had finished with his client. Now he came and stood over me, lifting my hair away from my face impatiently, taking over from the girl who had been fiddling uncertainly. He cut my hair very short, shaping it around my face and giving me an odd enquiring look. When he had finished, he looked at me in the mirror.

'Now you can see how pretty you are.'

The girl at reception who took my money, seeing how shocked I was at how much it cost, said, 'Do you know who just did your hair? That was Vidal Sassoon.'

I had arrived!

The neon advertising around Piccadilly Circus made the afternoon darker and louder as the traffic clogged the streets. Ahead of me was Shaftesbury Avenue and the West End. I did not have the courage to walk down that street past the imposing buildings. This was why I had come to London, to confront my fear of the theatre. It held for me a sad fascination as though if I were brave, that could define me.

Drawn by the sound of Big Ben I walked towards Trafalgar Square. Generations had left traces and the resonance of other times, as this great city continually reinvented itself. In the blank jigsaw of my life, I knew this was expected of me.

If I kept walking I could feed the pigeons and be a tourist. In front of me was a theatre, the billboards advertising a comedy. "A Hilarious Romp, Finest Performance Ever! Must See. Not To Be Missed". Large black and white words. The name of a play up in lights. An invitation.

The first play I saw was *Waiting for Gillian*. In the auditorium the noise subsided as the lights dimmed and the curtain went up on the stage, an empty space and meaningless words and meaningless actions. During the interval I went down the alley next to the theatre. The leading lady was sitting out on the fire escape, smoking. She was real, detached from the theatre and the play, alone in a way I had never experienced before. I have no idea why this marked me so profoundly. It finally became the demon I had to confront.

Chapter Two

The old man at the stage door sent me downstairs to see Stan; he was making tea. He looked up, waiting for me to speak.

'I want to work in the theatre.'

'Where do you come from?'

He indicated to my duffel bag.

'Ireland.'

I felt him hesitating. I wanted to defend myself, to say I was not Irish.

'When did you arrive?'

'Today, on the ferry.'

'You came on your own?'

'Yes.'

His question was rhetorical. It did not concern him.

'Would you like some tea?'

'Yes, please.'

He did not speak again until he had poured the tea for me.

'Sugar?'

'No, thank you.'

I reached out to take the mug of tea from him. I was very thirsty.

'Why don't you sit down?'

He sat in an old red chair, sipping his tea. Swivelling his chair round, he looked at me thoughtfully.

'Can you start tonight? Len phoned in to say he has another job, so he won't be on the auxiliary lighting board. If you want the job, it's yours?'

'Yes, thank you.'

I was too amazed to be surprised.

'It seems you came to the right place.'

He did not say this casually. It was as though he knew something unsaid. It really was as simple as that. To this day, Stan remains unchanged, ageless.

'Are you the new understudy?'

On my way back up the stairs I walked onto the empty stage. I could not see who was speaking because of the footlights.

'No.'

'Are you an actress?'

'No.'

'Oh, goodie, there are far too many of us already. Look at me my dear, a child star fallen into disuse.'

I thought, *I want to be...*

A dark-haired boy a little older than me walked out of the wings.

'I'm Jan. Who are you?'

'Nina.'

'Well, hi, Nian.'

I spent my first night in London sleeping in the old chair Stan used. Alfred, the doorman, found me in the morning and told me where I could find a bed-sit. Alfred knew about bed-sits; he had lived alone in one for thirty years. I caught the bus to Streatham, across the river where it was cheaper. Then I, like Alfred, moved into a room with a window, a gas heater and someone else's furniture. The first thing I did was to buy a red kettle for company. It's a strange thing about living alone; you have to be brave.

Now that I lived in London, at least most of my nights were taken care of. I was at the theatre, arriving in the early evening as the days became longer, dissolving the frozen winter I had left behind. I had tea with Stan and Pravin, who worked on the second auxiliary lighting board. Jan would call "overture" and "beginners please" over the speaker as the orchestra tuned their instruments before the curtain went up and the enthralled audience were captivated by the ceaseless magic. I knew in the deep recesses of my being that this was a happiness I would not have, ever being truly a part of this time. I carried within me the darkness and silence of a spectator, only living these events now as I chronicle them.

Chapter Three

'Look what I found.'

Jan came into the room under the stage with a young blonde boy. He was slight, his face tired and gentle. Pravin looked up from his book. He was going to creative writing classes. Jan told me with a mixture of envy and contempt that Pravin wanted to be an author.

'I've been explaining to Courtly I am resting.'

Jan filled the teapot with a flourish.

'That is what out-of-work actors do.'

He explained as he put the cups out.

'Now who wants tea?'

'I want a panda bear.'

'What kind of panda bear?'

'A six-foot panda bear.'

'Why?'

'So I can invent a life for him.'

'Why don't you invent a life for you?'

I knew nothing about me. Whenever I tried to imagine what it was I thought about, everything became vague, like a mirror that did not reflect me properly.

'Where did you get your name from?'

'Nina? From a play by Anton Chekhov, *The Seagull*. My father reads a lot.'

'I thought it was Nian.'

I shrugged.

'I am going to call you Nian. I don't want you to be a character in play.'

Then Jan went upstairs to take some tea to Alfred in his little cubbyhole at the stage door, Alfred who would shrivel up and die in daylight.

'How do you know Jan?'

The fair-haired boy turned and smiled. He seemed to shine.

'I met him at a party…'

He was beautiful: Courtly.

Jan and I would venture out into the cold to buy chestnuts roasting on the barrels. Then we would wander aimlessly around the streets between the matinée and the evening show. We had an imaginary six-foot panda bear to keep us company and we invented other lives so he would not leave us.

'Guess who I saw today?'

'Who?'

'That panda bear of yours, camp as a row of tents my dear, in love with a sailor.'

'Just my luck!'

Jan and I were walking down Oxford Street.

'Well, I hope it doesn't elope.'

'I meant to tell you, it's married.'

'To a sailor?'

I began to sing, 'A life on the ocean waves…'

'Hey, do you know that you have a nice voice?'

'What?'

'You should have your voice trained.'

It was raining, making the streets go all shiny so that I could see my reflection on the pavement. Jan pushed me into a shop. We were the only ones in there, except for a few plush people from the nether regions, or outer darkness as Jan called it. We were in Hamley's, floors and floors of toys. Jan left me to look around. He came back with a huge panda bear. My arms were full of it. I buried my face in its soft synthetic fur.

Chapter Four

I had not been to party for years. My parents whom I had abandoned had long since ceased to have any social interaction. My father was driving when the accident occurred and although he was exonerated by the law my mother was not so forgiving. A golden couple, rich, elegant, gliding effortlessly through life, had been abandoned by the society they were once part of. The concerned enquiries, flowers and cards ceased. Only Emily, my mother's sister who lived in Canada, remained constant. Injured in body and mind, my parents retreated into animosity and black depression, communicating with each other only through me; they had a go-between, so we as a family had no need of other people or entertainment.

The party was in the flat in Mayfair; Courtly, it seemed, moved in very exclusive circles. I had to tag along because of some industrial action I could not get across the river after the late show. It was quite crowded when we arrived. Courtly was generally kissed by everyone as he wore Jan like a love button. Boy, did I stand out in a crowd. I definitely did not belong with fashionably dressed young men with long hair and bright clothes as they flouted convention. Courtly came over to me where I huddled near the curtains.

'Well, if it is not the lost boy?'

'Hello, Gladys.'

Gladys kissed Courtly extravagantly, holding out a heavily ringed hand in my direction.

'And who is this?'

'Nian.'

Gladys raised an eyebrow.

'Your real name?'

'No.'

I felt lighter saying that.

'Very posh, I approve. Gladys is not the moniker I would have chosen, far too common.'

I laughed. Gladys and Courtly drifted into groups of different people.

'You came with Courtly?'

The well-modulated voice fitted his clothes. Dark slacks and a white open-neck shirt. He was scrupulously anonymous.

'I'm glad Courtly has a friend.'

The dim lighting smoothed his features. All his life he'd been careful, now he was with Courtly; it unsettled me.

Someone had just arrived, dressed all in black and sporting a pork pie hat; he made a dramatic entrance. This was met with shouted comments and laughter.

'Who invited the wallflower?'

I shrank, but he was looking at Gladys.

'Don't be bitchy, Ralf dear, it is so unbecoming.'

There was a lull, then he turned his back on Gladys, deliberately, rudely as he tossed his hat into the room to a round of applause.

The music had been turned up. I felt as though I was being fractured, I was breaking into pieces. Everything dissolved into sound. Outside, on the landing, I could breathe again.

'Bloody hell!'

Gladys almost tripped over me in the gloom.

'Why don't you go home?'

'I don't want to be alone.'

'Who does, dear?'

Gladys sat next to me on the step, adjusting the wig that had slipped down with a comic gesture.

'It's all getting a bit much, the effort to be me.'

I sighed, it was very late and I was tired.

'I hope you're not waiting for Courtly, lost boys never go home.'

'When I was a child I was always terrified of the crocodile in *Peter Pan*. He was called Tick-Tock because he had swallowed a clock.'

Gladys glanced sideways at me.

'It's not the crocodile you have the fear, it's the clock. Tick-tock and you are old.'

Beneath the make-up, lines were showing. The jawline had slackened, thickening into a double chin. I had no understanding of age as I looked away from the tired eyes.

'Promise me you will never grow old, darling.'

I rested against Gladys.

'I promise.'

And the party went on without us.

Tick-tock.

It was cold outside and very quiet. I sort of held Jan up until we found a taxi to Bayswater where he lived in a bed-sit. He didn't say anything until we were in bed together.

'Where do you live?'

'Other side of the river.'

'You have to move closer…'

He was falling asleep when he said, 'To me.'

It was the first time in my life I had been in bed with someone. Jan put his arms around me. He smelled sweet, lulled and comforted I shut my eyes and went to sleep, the gentle rest of the pure.

A few weeks later, we all moved into Pravin's terraced house in Putney, we being Jan, Courtly, and Sometime the panda bear. Oh, and me too. Pravin's parents had died withering away in the cold and strangeness of their adopted country, working many hours in a little corner shop. When he was little, Pravin had been looked after by a Scottish spinster he called his Auntie. She had lived next to their shop and read to him the books of her childhood to fill the emptiness of being alone. Then Pravin's mother died and he had had to leave school to help his father in the shop. Now with no parents and hated shop sold, Pravin was determined to have a new life. He had been studying for two years for his A-levels. He wanted to be educated and that, to Pravin, meant university. He needed us to subsidise that ambition. Pravin did not want to be a famous novelist by recreating his past. Jan helped me paint my room white because Jan said I reminded him of a nun. Courtly ruthlessly discarded what he called clutter, the remnants of Pravin's family. Courtly had been disowned by his father the moment he had ventured out of the closet. Courtly's father as a second-generation army man had had great expectations.

That first Sunday, we had coffee in what used to be Pravin's parents' bedroom. The only things to remind us that they had ever lived there was their double bed, the statue of the elephant god, Ganesh, brass candle sticks and a stepladder that had been left in the middle of the kitchen. It never occurred to any of us to move it. Now Jan and Courtly were lying on their bed using Sometime as a pillow. I sat with my feet on the bed, drinking hot coffee. Pravin came in with a mug of tea. His religion did not allow him to smoke or drink.

'It must be funny having to share your house with lodgers?'

I think Jan felt awkward lolling on what used to be Pravin's parents' bed.

'You are my friends. I am glad to share my house.'

Jan got up. He took the statue of Ganesh and put it in the front room with the brass candle sticks making a small altar on the mantelpiece. Courtly insisted we draw the curtains so we could light the candles. The flames came up warm against my lips. I put out my tongue trying to taste it.

'Are you putting a spell on us?'

'Yes, I'm wishing.'

'What did you wish for?' Courtly asked.

I didn't know what to wish for. I shut my eyes briefly.

Chapter Five

I decided to have singing lessons. I had my grandmother's legacy, the money that had enabled me to leave Ireland. In it, my grandmother had stipulated it was be used to fund my further education. I had stayed with my grandmother, rattling around in her large house when my parents were away, travelling abroad for my father's business. I was always afraid that if I were not very good, they would not come back for me.

When the phone rang one morning, my grandmother listened without speaking for some time. Her voice was quite calm when she asked,

'Are they alive?'

I knew then something awful had happened.

'Your parents have been involved in a terrible accident. They are both gravely injured.'

I ran sobbing to my grandmother for comfort but she stopped me, saying,

'Don't cry. It's a sign of defeat.'

I have lived with that stern injunction ever since.

My music teacher lived in a dark basement flat. I walked past the overflowing dustbin and rang the bell. A tall man opened the door; he seemed to stoop when he saw me.

'How can I help you?'

'Can you teach me to sing?'

'That depends. Do you have a voice?'

Before I could answer, he went down the dusty passage into a room scattered with sheet music and a piano. The radio was on. He turned to me.

'Music is my passion. It is the way to the soul.'

He went over to the piano and without sitting down played a scale, the sound intruding into the cluttered room.

'You want your voice trained. Why?'

'To be visible.'

He sighed.

'Turn the radio off. Can you do that?'

Without that sound, we were frighteningly alone. He sat down at the piano. This time the scale was different, longer.

'Sing.'

'Again.'

The scales went up and down and then up and up. His hands were still on the keys.

'You have the natural octave range of an opera singer.'

Not that I ever doubted I was brilliant, but it's nice to have your worst fears confirmed.

Luca, as he asked his foreign students to call him, lived alone with his piano and radio. He was a political refugee from Czechoslovakia. There had been a lot in the news about the Russian invasion. Now he hunched over the coffee he made for us, listening to the BBC World Service, desperate for news.

'I am sorry. I hope you do not mind the radio. I keep it on to hear other voices. My mother taught me English. She wanted me to know a language of the west.'

His face, with its neatly trimmed beard, was drawn and sad.

'Do you still live with your parents?'

'No.'

He held his coffee carefully in his hands.

'Remember, family is everything.'

I took a deep breath. I felt as though I had been found guilty of something and I needed to defend myself. I wanted to explain to Luca why I did not live with my parents.

'They don't talk to me.'

'So you come here and sing so you can be heard.'

I didn't want him burdened with any more sadness, so I laughed and said,

'Yes, you have to listen to me.'

Luca seemed to see me for the very first time. He nodded as though confirming something he remembered.

'I heard a song on the radio – *San Francisco*. I liked it very much. Do you know it?'

Of course I knew it. I was always singing it with Courtly.

'I only have the sheet music given to me from the British Council. Western music is new to me.'

I sang *San Francisco*, not just for Luca but because it encapsulated so much of this time.

Chapter Six

Courtly did not come back one night. The drama! Jan had us knee-deep in tears. The actors had to dog paddle onto stage. I kept making tea for Jan because he was getting dehydrated. Pravin developed writers' cramp and had nothing to say as he retreated behind *War and Peace*.

Jan went to bed with Sometime. At about I don't know what time, I woke up. It was Courtly.

'Who has Jan got in bed with him?'

'Someone he picked up on the Putney Towpath.'

'Whoever it is, they have a backside the size of the Queen Mary.'

'Serves you right. Where were you anyway?'

Courtly was quiet for a long time, which was unusual for him.

'Oh God!'

He began to whimper.

'Come to bed.'

Courtly pulled off his clothes and crept into bed beside me. I held him close to stop his shivering.

'What happened?'

'Someone went mad. He went mad. Wham!'

'How?'

'We were tripping.'

'What?'

'Tripping, you know, taking LSD.'

'Well, you're crazy.'

'Not me, Charlie Brown. Sing to me.'

'What?'

'Sing a rainbow.'

He was pretty bombed, so I sang.

Courtly went to sleep a little while after that.

Courtly was still asleep in my bed in the afternoon. Not wanting to disturb him, I tagged along with Pravin to his creative writing classes. The institute he went to offered a range of other classes. I left Pravin and wandered into a big empty room. I was sitting on the table near the window when other people started to wander in. He, the drama tutor, did not know that I was not included in the class because he had been asked to fill in for another teacher.

When I was small, I played the part of a milkmaid in my school play. I had one line.

My parents were not there to see me. I remembered forever the sharp joy of being someone else. At the end of the class, I went up to him. The afternoon had faded outside the big windows.

'Do you take private students?'

'Yes.'

'Can you teach me?'

There was a tiny hesitation as though we held our breath.

'Yes.'

I had taken a step without meaning to.

'Do you know Dineley's Studios? They are off Baker Street. I will book a room for next Tuesday at four o'clock.'

I did not want to be an actress. But I had to do something brave. If I did not, I would be lost. Now I was going to be taught to act, me who could not even cry.

Chapter Seven

After I began having acting lessons I would wake up with the feeling as if I had fallen into the sky. Even before I opened my eyes, it would be there, an endless void I was lost in. Normality did not agree with me nor did my drama lessons. I arrived early at the rehearsal room. I was sitting on the floor, hugging my knees against me when my private tutor came in. He was a quiet, remote man who watched me patiently with his distant kindness, willing me to do something I could not grasp. I did not get up when he came in.

'Can you tell me what the matter is?'

He took my hands, kneeling next to me.

He was so gentle, so concerned. It was the first time, for as long as I could remember of anyone showing me care.

'I don't know how to be here.'

He stood up and walked to the window.

'When you asked me to teach you, you were asking for help. It was such a cry from the heart. I found it irresistible.'

He understood. I had jumped into the dark and he had been there to catch me.

'You should consider going to The Tavistock Clinic. They have some very good people. They might be able to help you. You should not feel the way you do.'

'I had a sad childhood.'

I was glib. I had to protect myself. No one must ever know me.

'It's nice to see you smiling. I want you to start applying to drama schools. You need structure in your life, a roof over your head.'

I was briefly safe and protected.

'You're so bright.'

He put out his hand and softly traced the outline of my face with his fingertips, his eyes very attentive and encompassing me, oddly sad. I wanted to reach out to him but I had nothing to give him except all the years until I understood.

The very first audition I went to involved two set pieces, one of them from Shakespeare and the other from Harold Pinter. Three men and two women sat in a darkened auditorium at a table with a shielded light. One of them said,

'Begin when you are ready.'

'Take your time.'

I was an impostor standing there. I did not love the theatre. I had no ambition. The only reason I was doing this was to prove I had courage. As I started speaking the lines, Harold Pinter's lines, they became mine.

'Thank you for coming.'

'We will let you know.'

I walked off the stage. I was so defeated, so destroyed. I was surprised I could still feel the pain in my heart. The next day I opened the letter.

'We regret we are unable to offer you...'

After I failed the first couple of auditions, I sort of went into traumatic shock. I took to wearing make-up, something I had never done before or since. Armed with my death mask, I set out to conquer the world's next oldest profession. It was all incredibly dramatic stuff. I massacred Juliet, the bride in *Blood Wedding*, and *The Duchess of Malfi*, all in the space of about six weeks.

The only thing that gave me the courage to do this was the fact the playwright would remain forever a stranger and could not judge me as I spoke his words. Then they would say, their voices coming from somewhere in the darkened auditorium.

'Thank you. We will let you know.'

And you knew you had failed.

For my last audition I wore jeans and no make-up. I had chosen a piece from a comedy, someone laughed. I was accepted at once.

27

Chapter Eight

Courtly insisted on making a dress for me to wear on my first day at drama school, using the sewing machine in our little room under the stage. Jan bought some pink and red material, the sort you make towels out of. In the age of the mini, it just about covered my arse. No one looked any different to me, except they were not wearing a beach towel. There were twenty-six of us being ignored and overlooked. We huddled together in a long room, waiting for the first class to begin.

The first day at drama school, I felt as though I had ceased to exist except for sorrow. That cold day in a pale empty sky filled me with such sadness. All that long day when knowledge was opened up to me, I felt my heart breaking. I could never allow myself to succeed. God must have been somewhere once, for me to have felt so forsaken that day.

My drama school from the start was a battlefield. We were asked to improvise the characters and situation we were given to help us understand the meaning behind the text. Faced with this I was dumb.

Mila and Ben loved the freedom of exploring their emotions, drawing on their youth and assurance. The tutors here did not accept anyone who had just left school believing that they needed some life experience; mine had been to be invisible. Now I was improvising the hidden text of a play exploring mental instability, for laid-back Ben and Mila, this was opportunity because they were not using drama school as a form of therapy. I must have been crazy even to attempt this. It was perfect casting.

I sometimes joined my class in the school canteen, listening to the latest gossip – who had been laid, who fancied whom. I was not privy to their lives as they formed friendships, shared flats, spent time in bed-sits smoking pot and drinking coffee. Without my being aware of it, they, the group I worked with every day, were colouring me.

One morning, I collided with someone coming out of the bathroom.

'Oh, who are you?'

I pushed past him without bothering to answer.

'Knock, can't you?'

Courtly sat up in bed.

'Who is that in the…?'

'Bog.'

Courtly sighed and lay down again, pulling the bedclothes around him. At this point, he drifted back into the room.

'Allow me to introduce you to Paul. Paul this is Nian.'

Jan was sitting on the stepladder in the kitchen, using Sometime's ears to wipe his eyes.

'You're crazy! He's not worth it.'

'I love him.'

What can you say to that?

'Who you waiting for?'

'I'll know when I meet him.'

'Like Sometime.'

'Yes, you gave him to me.'

Paul came waltzing into the kitchen.

'Pardon me! I seem to be breaking up the happy home.'

Paul was older than us. His very short hair made him look like an out-of-uniform marine. I hoped Paul would be fat and bald by the time he was forty. Underneath the sheet he was wearing, he was beginning to sag; in his world, he was almost buried before he was dead.

I got to school early, the canteen had not opened, so I went and sat next to the radiator in the cloakroom. Abby came in. She was not in our group. She was tall and thin and that made her stand out.

'Do you know where I can get an abortion?'

I did not know how to get pregnant. But I answered politely.

'No, I am sorry I don't.'

The scattered convents I had gone to never mentioned sex. The only advice we were given was to be good. I had taken that to heart. I was always obedient.

'Did you get in on your first audition?' she asked abruptly.

'Yes.'

She was at the mirror, putting on her make-up.

'I auditioned for two years before I was accepted.'

I didn't know if I was guilty or entitled.

'What would you do if you got knocked up?'

How do you answer that when you are a hundred-year-old virgin in a permissive society?

She turned from the mirror to look at me critically.

'Do you have a bloke?'

'No.'

'She glanced back with an expression of distaste and shrugged.

'They should make abortion legal. Then I wouldn't have this hassle. I should have the right to choose.'

She looked back at herself in the mirror, satisfied with the effect of the black eyeliner, picked up her bag and went out.

The last class of the day was cancelled. Morris, a boy in my class, suggested we go to his place – instant coffee and pot in some bed-sit.

'Take your coat off.'

When the others had gone off to the pub, I had stayed. I was beginning to feel pleasantly bombed. It turned out to be quite a night.

It was cold and when Morris suggested getting into bed, I agreed. It was so strange to have someone expecting me to respond to a demand being made on my body. It seemed rather comical at first. Then it all went wrong and I started to feel sad. I got out of bed and began to put my clothes on.

'What's the matter?'

'Nothing! I've changed my mind. That's all.'

'What's wrong? Is it me?'

This kind of conversation can go on all night.

'I told you I changed my mind.'

'Why?'

See what I mean.

'It's got nothing to do with you.'

'Are you a virgin, or something?'

I let it hang there both figuratively and literally.

'You'll catch cold standing there. Come back to bed.'

I felt stupid, as if I was making a fuss over nothing. So, I got back into bed but his conversation kept drifting back to what he very definitely had on his mind.

'Why do you think it's wrong for you to sleep with me?'

Talk about a stupid expression. Of course, I would sleep with him, but he was looking for a screw and that was not going to be me.

'Being with me is not going to hurt anyone, is it?'

'Yes, it would hurt me.'

'How?'

But it would take too long to explain; it was impossible to stay in bed with him. So, in the end, I slept on the sofa. I woke up very early in the morning. I had missed out on the experience that would have meant I was part of the scene. But, if I was to be made up of memories, a fuck from a randy boy in my class was probably not one I wanted.

Chapter Nine

We spent hours at the zoo studying the animals. I was glad to be part of our group, to belong to the school. I had purpose and direction, a roof over my head. At first, we just wondered about feeling important as though we were wearing a uniform that identified us as drama students. Clea stopped in front of the lion enclosure.

'I would love to be the king of the jungle.'

She opened her eyes wide, bringing her hands up in a mock roar.

'No one would be able to hurt me ever again.'

She took my arm as we walked on.

'When my Nan died I was taken into care. I don't know why they call it "care"; no one cares about you. It's all rules and punishment and perverts. So I ran away with Jake.'

She stopped walking and turned to me.

'Now I am going to be actress.'

'Yes.'

She gave her funny quirky grin and, laughing, she wandered away from me, mingling with the visitors to the zoo.

I expected most of them would be attracted by the big important animals but I was wrong. They were little grey birds flying free, wary of being caged. The polar bear paced helplessly in the barren concrete enclosure, turning his head looking, not seeing, and knowing it was hopeless. All I had to do was copy the movements. Those sunny autumn days bound me to this small group of people as we walked under the falling leaves.

The tutors assessed our efforts. The criterion was that they could identify our chosen animal. It was all very casual. We sat in the auditorium and watched as one by one we presented our animals. Clea had us all laughing helplessly of her interpretation of a penguin.

The animal Belle had chosen was a timid, skittish deer so accurately observed, yet with an insistence that she was acknowledged.

I watched with fascination as Talia slowly transformed herself into a python, each movement calculated, unfolding into the next, I expected applause; then it was my turn.

'For someone so slight, we were impressed that you chose such a heavy animal.'

I had passed!

The rest of the school was beginning to empty as we struggled with the play we were studying, trying to unlock the characters we had been given. I was deadly afraid I would not be able to contain my terror at exploring their madness. Clea was watching me from across room; she winked as she walked slowly over to me. We had not really spoken since the day at the zoo when she told me about the bad boy, Jake, she had run away with. Clea made me think of a black and white picture of a film star with her mass of bleach blonde curls. The rosebud pout outlined the deep red lipstick. She came and perched on one of the many props I brought to school to act as a buffer between me and the people I worked with.

'I had a strange experience last night. I was waiting to get the tube. It was late, so there was just this man on the platform and me. I thought he was flasher because he kept on staring at me then he said, "Do you always wear your grandmother's wedding ring?" It really freaked me out. I had gloves on.'

Clea was wearing a beaten silver band with a row of brass bells. She put her hand up to them with a small shudder.

'I hope they protect me.'

'They will.'

My voice sounded hollow, an echo of a wish for her.

She stood up and gave me a quick hug.

'Don't look so sad, or you will make me cry.'

Chapter Ten

At last, the term was grinding to an end and Christmas was coming. Not that I ever set much store by Christmas but this would be the first one away from home. I went shopping with my carefully hoarded money, joining the other savages in the frantic rush of the last of the Christians. Paul was still with us – worse luck. The bedding arrangements in the house had changed quite a lot. Courtly was enchanted with Paul, so Jan had moved in with me. Sometime took up residence in the kitchen propped up on the stepladder. Pravin, still busy writing his eternal novel, was hiding from us in a house that had once been his home.

The phone rang. It was a man for Courtly. He was not pleased when I answered the phone.

'Hello, is Courtly there?'

'Who shall I say is calling?'

'Is he there?'

Boy, he rattled easily.

'No, may I take a message?'

'I'll call again.'

He hung up. I kept trying to imagine what they did in bed together.

'Someone called for you.'

Courtly was floating around the room with a hairdryer.

'Your lover just phoned.'

I shouted to get his attention. He turned the hairdryer off.

'What did he want?'

'You.'

Courtly blew me a kiss.

'Did he leave a message?'

'No.'

'Of course not,' he said patting his nice little rump.

'I'm jail bait.'

He put the hairdryer down.

'I've got a present for my mother.'

Are you going to give it to her?'

'I will have to go and see her when my father is not there.'

'Otherwise he will throw you out of the house?'

'That really broke my mother's heart.'

Courtly was quiet for a long time before he spoke, because he was sad.

'Do you know, Nian? Sometimes when we are in the street together, I pretend you are my girlfriend.'

I kissed him and the afternoon faded into darkness.

The school finally closed for the Christmas holidays. Swinging London had mostly done the trendy thing and abandoned old-fashioned traditions of peace and goodwill. John Lennon was right, *The Beatles* were more popular than Christ.

Jan went shopping in the morning. He came back with a small Christmas tree and presents for all of us.

'Do you think Ganesh minds us having a Christmas tree?' Jan asked.

'He does not mind.'

Pravin looked around wistfully.

'I wish I could stay and have Christmas here, but my Auntie is all alone.'

'Like my dad. That's why I always spend Christmas with him,' Jan agreed.

I mourned my family, my mother and father trapped in their silence. I sent a Christmas card with my address, my gift in an empty crib.

Courtly came back late in the afternoon with lights for the Christmas tree. Jan had already gone to catch the train down to Surrey.

'Hello, Purity.' Paul called out, kissing Courtly as he came into the kitchen. I kept hoping one day Paul would be gone.

'Listen, Paul, if you are going to live here, you better pay in some money.'

'Jesus! Who runs this place?'

Paul looked at Courtly, affronted.

'I'm sick of you free loading off us.'

'She's so butch, isn't she?'

Courtly laughed.

'If you think it's so funny, then you better find yourself at the paid end of a night cruise so you can feed Paul and pay his share of the rent.'

'She's such a bitch.'

Paul leaned against the kitchen door vamping Courtly blowing him a kiss.

Courtly winked back at Paul.

'Jealousy will get you nowhere.'

Then they flounced out of the kitchen where Pravin was pottering about making tea.

'Does Courtly really do that, take money?'

What planet was Pravin on?

Pravin held the cup very carefully, looking at me, waiting for an answer.

'No.'

Then Pravin went out into the dark winter afternoon to catch the train to Scotland.

I went to the market down the North End Road to get coconut brittle for Courtly and to look for a winter coat that I really needed. I saw Abby wandering about alone, aimlessly.

'Do you live near here?'

She showed no surprise when she saw me.

'Yes, in Putney.'

She looked sort of battered, thinner.

'Happy Christmas.'

Abby glanced at me with disbelief, startled.

'Oh,' she gave a funny little laugh, 'I had forgotten it is Christmas.'

I didn't want to go back to the house. The only thing I could do when it was so cold was to go to the cinema, me and all the lonely people. I can still remember the bitter taste of wrapping myself in myself against the cold. I had to be a good soldier, because the hardest was the best. By the time I understood why I believed this, I would have probably missed the boat and would spend the rest of my life in a half-empty cinema.

Chapter Eleven

Courtly said he had a surprise for us. I will say this for his surprise; it certainly made for a memorable Christmas. Paul and Courtly were doing LSD and I was not into that. I would have liked to have gone to bed but a feeling of unease stopped me, so I picked Sometime up and dozed with him in my arms, my head on the kitchen table.

Someone was sobbing softly next to me. Someone kept sobbing and sobbing. I was suddenly wide-awake and looking at Courtly. He had cut his wrists. I made him sit down and bound his wrists tightly with tea towels and then I wrapped a blanket around him. The bleeding stopped. Courtly had made a mess of cutting his wrists. He was not going to die. I could not leave him alone, lost somewhere on some God-forsaken trip. It was such a long night. It began to get light far away from us. Courtly was still whimpering softly, monotonously. Jesus wept. Courtly wept. I was too tired and cold to think about anything except that this was Christmas day.

Paul came drifting in at about ten.

'Is he still at it? He's such a drama queen.'

God, I hated him.

'Get out.'

'How was I to know that such a major junkie can't handle a trip?'

'Get out.'

'No need to throw a frothy.'

'You're such a cunt.'

'You should know.'

'Pimp.'

'You're pathetic.'

I locked myself in the loo, shutting myself away from Paul, afraid he would take my soul.

It was late afternoon when Courtly escaped from the magic mushrooms.

'I'm hungry.'

'How do you feel?'

'Fine.'

Courtly let me wash and undress him. Paul had gone. I took the mattress off Pravin's bed and put it in front of the television, taking Sometime out of the kitchen so we would not be alone, falling asleep to the sound of canned laughter. Well, if that was Christmas, it was over.

I bought Courtly a silver wrist chain with a flat silver tag with his name engraved on it in case he got lost. Now Courtly was out somewhere on this very cold night, hoping some rich man would want a blowjob so he could get his next fix.

On old year's night I went to the theatre, to the comfort of Stan who accepted my presence there without comment. The theatre had installed a new lighting board, so we were no longer needed. Stan gave me tea from the pot he had made, drinking his in his old red chair. From under the stage, we could hear the low rumble of the actors and the muffled sound of the audience laughing and the applause at the curtain call. Tonight, Alfred could not face being alone in his bed-sit with all his family gone. I remember him talking about his mum who had been dead forever and Big Ben chiming in the New Year.

Chapter Twelve

Jan's father had given him money for Christmas and Jan decided to cast his bread upon the waters and go to Holland with Courtly.

'Why Amsterdam?'

'Gayest City there is, my dear. Jan was born there.'

'You don't say. I would never have guessed it.'

'What's the matter with you?' Courtly demanded.

'Sour grapes,' I said, because it was true.

'When are you going?'

'In two days' time.'

'You're certainly not letting the grass grow under your feet.'

'Listen to it, my dear. It's more packed with clichés than the agony column in Woman's Own.'

Jan put his arms around me.

'Will you be alright?'

'Yes. Anyhow, Pravin going to be here, isn't he?'

'Perhaps he will lose all his inhibitions and bring a bird back while we are away.'

'I think Pravin prefers a bird in the hand to one in the bush.'

Courtly suggested archly.

Jan laughed.

'It will be nice showing Courtly around.'

'Make sure you bring him back.'

Courtly smiled and kissed the top of my head.

They left early in the morning. I closed the door behind them, took Sometime and got back into bed. Courtly had painted the ceiling in my room black and strung the Christmas lights above my bed. I had come back late from school to find them there, winking away on the ceiling. 'Now you can have Christmas every day if you want,' Courtly had explained.

They were winking on and off when Pravin came in with some coffee.

'What happened over Christmas?'

'Nothing.'

'Why did Paul go?'

I wished Pravin disapproved more of what was happening in his house instead of sounding so unsure.

'It's just as well Paul has gone. Paul is a dealer. I don't fancy having the fuzz around for tea and no sympathy.'

'Fuzz?'

I am quite convinced that Pravin was writing a novel about non-communication, whatever that is.

A week later Jan phoned in tears, Courtly had been on a really bad trip. They could not do the long ferry journey. I wired them the money to come back by plane. My grandmother would not have approved of her money being used for people who were not mentioned in polite society.

'Do you like watching the planes?'

I had gone to the airport to meet Jan and Courtly when they got back. I went to the window of the terminal to watch the planes take off and land.

'Are you waiting for someone?'

He was standing next to me at the window. Unsure of how long it took to get to Heathrow I was early.

'Yes.'

'And you?'

'I have a plane to catch to America.'

'I would love to go to America.'

'Do all young people want to go to America?'

'No.'

'Oh, I see, you're special.'

I smiled and he smiled back.

He took my arm and guided me into the lounge.

'Are you a student?'

'I'm going to be an actress.'

He burst out laughing. The drinks came; he raised his glass to me.

'Skol.'

The Campari looked like raspberry and tasted like gall. I pulled a face. He smiled, this time only with his lips.

"Swinging London", is it really swinging London?'

'Sometimes.'

'You like London?'

'I love London. It's my city.'

It was, as it sprawled vast and grey all around me, that day and always.

They announced the Pan American flight to New York.

'You can come with me and say goodbye.'

I walked with him to the customs area.

'It was nice speaking to you.'

He bowed slightly.

'Say hello to New York for me when you get there.'

He started to go through the barrier, stopping to fill in a form. He turned and came back to where I was standing.

'My card, my name is Anton.'

He handed it to me, oddly diffident.

'You can write to me. I would like that.'

I took the card.

'Yes.'

'You promise?'

It was light-hearted.

'Yes.'

'A promise is a promise.'

'I promise.'

Chapter Thirteen

Jan came through arrivals with his arm around Courtly who did not recognise me.

We got the coach from the terminus. On the tube, Courtly began whimpering.

Jan put his hands over his face.

'Make him stop please, Nian. Please make him stop.'

I put my arms around Courtly.

'It's all right. It's all right.'

Those were words I could not say before, words that were not true.

I put Courtly to bed with all his clothes on. Jan stood in the kitchen.

'Should we get a doctor?'

'I have to go back to school.'

'Please don't leave me, please.'

'I have to go to school.'

I went, leaving them to go back to that ridiculous world of make-believe.

Courtly was strung out and looking for a fix, and I was in my practice skirt playing the role of Belle's mother. We did not often work together in pairs or do improvisations based on our lives. Belle described her mother to me and the situation at home.

That was not my mother but I understood what it was like to be implacable.

Her defiance and bravado finally dissolved into tears.

Then it was my turn. I had never defied anyone.

'What's your mother like?'

'Disfigured.'

She took my hands.

'Can you do this?'

I shook my head as she waited for me to speak.

'No.'

All the classrooms were occupied, so we went outside.

'Was it a bad scene?'

'Yes.'

'Did you tell them?'

'No.'

'Perhaps you should?'

I hugged my knees against me. It was a cold afternoon. She looked over at me, concerned.

'Do you want to go inside?'

I shook my head.

'You never say much. Do you talk to anyone?'

'Yes, Jemma. She calls me the Mother Superior.'

'It's not meant to be flattering.'

She was teasing.

'I know.'

I smiled at her.

'Remember how scared we all were on the first day?'

'I still am.'

'Don't take it all too seriously.'

She got up.

'They do want the best for us.'

I went back to watch the improvisations.

The lesson ended. The class broke up, drifting towards the canteen.

Belle came up to me and wrapped a large colourful shawl around me.

'Remember, you are one of us.'

The language of the heart.

When I got back, Jan was not there. Courtly was. He had taken some downers and was scarily calm.

'Do you know where Jan is?'

'Am I my brother's keeper?'

'Don't, Nian, please.'

'I don't know where Jan is.'

Courtly was crouching on the bed. I sat down next to him, putting my arms around him because I was sad and also afraid.

'I think Jan is going to leave.'

'Why?' I asked because I agreed with him.

'Amsterdam was really something.'

'Oh, who were you screwing?'

'I had a really bad trip.'

'Why do you do it?'

'Christ! What a question.'

I got up.

'Would you like some tea?'

'No.'

'No, thank you.'

He looked up and smiled wanly.

'I am going to die.'

'We all are.'

'No, I'm going to die.'

Why couldn't they go away like tourists and come back and tell me about the tulips and windmills. If they wanted a trip, they could have stayed here.

'No, Courtly.'

'That's not my real name.'

'What is your name?'

'Charles.'

'Prince Charles is one thing, my dear, but Queen Charles!'

We both laughed, with the days past irrevocably lost to us.

Chapter Fourteen

Jan was waiting for me outside the school. I was surprised to see him. He had drifted away from us since Amsterdam. Some of my class came out and called 'good night' as they went past me as the warm tide.

'Are any of them any good?' Jan asked looking after them.

'Yes.'

'Who?'

'Me.'

We began to walk away from the school.

'The drug scene in Holland is really heavy. I think that's why Courtly wanted to go there.'

'I thought it was you who wanted to go to Holland?'

'No, Courtly did. I didn't want him to go back to Paul.'

'You won't go and leave us, will you?'

Jan sounded weary.

'Go where?'

'Well, you are sort of our mother.'

'That's because I am an old maid.'

'I bet there are lots of virgins in your class.'

'I bet there are not.'

'The first time I had sex was with an extra on a film shoot. I had a small part. You didn't know I had been in a film?' Jan laughed and winked, then became serious, trying to understand how it had all come to this.

'He adored me. I thought he was big joke. His whole life was hanging around film sets being an extra. We all knew he was a fag. Some of the cast used to tell me to keep away from him. In the end, I seduced him.'

'Why?'

'I wanted to humiliate him. I hated the fact he obsessed over me. "I just adore you. You're so beautiful." Can you imagine hearing that from this pathetic old queen? Besides, I was a randy boy and I was curious. So, I discovered the awful truth. And look at me now, my dear, bent as boomerang. My mother guessed. She said, "Don't let papa ever find out. It will hurt him too much."'

Jan lost in remembering what his mother had said, hesitated as we passed the tube station.

'Would you like to meet Robert?'

I knew about Robert. Jan had met him in Amsterdam. Robert had just finished at art school and had been in Amsterdam to complete his portfolio. The trouble was he added Jan to it. Jan stopped walking and turned to me.

'It was a really bad scene. Courtly was out of it most of the time.'

He went on with a small shudder.

'I was so scared when he disappeared. I didn't know what had happened to him. Robert helped me find him. I would have been pretty sunk without Robert.'

I wanted Robert to go away so Jan would come back.

'Robert lives with Geoff, who is an art critic. Geoff is going to help Robert with his exhibition. He was voted the young artist of the year at his art school.'

'I'm surprised you didn't elope with dear Robert.'

'Why don't you ever go home, Nian?'

'Because.'

'Don't they miss you?'

I could think of nothing to say.

'My dad lives in Surrey; you could come with me to visit him. We could go down by train.'

Jan glanced at me, unsure.

'He knows that I'm gay.'

I heard his sadness as though he had broken a promise to his mother.

'That's good.'

'Why?'

'Because it doesn't matter.'

Jan smiled at me then.

'Papa will like you.'

The house, once we got inside, really needed a nice butch influence like me. It was all white and purple. We went into a green wood-panelled kitchen where Geoff was fluttering around in the kitchen.

'Hello, Jan. We were just about to have tea,' Geoff mentioned, ignoring me.

'Hello, Robert,' Jan said quietly. Robert, who was sitting in the corner, stood up. He was slim, with classically sculpted features. He must have been older than we were to be so exhausted already. 'Have some tea. Geoff's just made it,' Robert motioned to Geoff dismissively.

'I don't know. I seem to be nothing but the hand maiden,' Geoff retorted as he bustled about.

The soft light in the kitchen was smothering.

'Tea?'

Geoff proffered the teapot in my direction.

I don't like tea and strange houses and critics. Robert asked Jan to look at his new painting. Geoff and I were left, blank and shut up in our own hostility. I could smell Geoff's after-shave from where he sat, loveless and worn out in the concealed lighting in his kitchen.

Chapter Fifteen

Lyn, who so absorbed into the school that I hardly knew her, was having a party and, for some reason, I was invited with the rest of them. Lyn lived with Adam who seemed to have only one talent, scoring hash for anyone who wanted it. We had tea and cake. Someone had made a birthday cake with lots of cherries and nuts and hash. I only realised how much shit there was in that cake when I floated out with the rest of them to join the Anti-Vietnam War march on a sunny afternoon.

There were thousands of people massed at Trafalgar Square holding red banners and chanting "Stop USA bombs" and "Peace in Vietnam".

We walked peacefully, guided by stewards. I got caught up in a group of people that suddenly broke away and was pushed along with them. A line of police in their blue uniforms stood in front of the American Embassy. An angry mob rushed forward, refusing to be stopped, scattering the police cordon.

A scuffle broke out close to me. Mounted police were moving forward, trying to push us back. Adam took an aerosol can out of his jacket pocket, aiming the spray into the face of the horse so close to me that I could feel its warm breath. The horse reared up, panicked. The young police officer fell, blood staining the road. Bottles and stones were being thrown.

Someone picked up a fallen banner, and, using the wooden pole, hit the horse very hard across its legs. I saw the horse's panic, fear and us, reflected in one large brown eye.

Almost everyone had gone. Normal traffic was moving down the street. I saw again the eye of the horse and knew that we had violated something sacred; the afternoon unravelled into a time that could not be fixed.

The house was empty when I got back. I ran a bath using almost all of Courtly's expensive bubble bath. I heard someone come in; Courtly was standing in the doorway, a dark blue cap with gold braid perched jauntily on his head.

'Oh, I see,' he said eyeing all the bubbles.

'What do you want?'

The effect of all that shit was wearing off. I could talk again.

'I want you to meet someone.'

Behind him, an airline pilot, impeccably dressed in his uniform, said,

'Pleased to meet you.'

'I'm taking the evening flight to Miami with Kevin. Aren't you going to say anything?'

'No, I'm stoned.'

I had lost a huge bit of me and allowed myself to be part of a mindless act.

Courtly's voice was somewhere in the bright light of the bathroom as he whispered,

'Don't you think he's gorgeous?'

Chapter Sixteen

'Good morning.'

I opened my eyes. Jan was smiling as he handed me a big mug of coffee.

'I put cream in it for you. I took Pravin some tea. He was really chuffed.'

I thought about Pravin waking up every morning alone and Jan making tea for him.

'You look very posh.'

'Geoff knows someone who works in telly. He said he might be able to get me some work. Just think, I could be making a comeback.'

'Really?'

I wasn't enthusiastic about it.

'Robert is going to an out-of-town art exhibition today.'

'Oh, is he any good?'

'Yes, he's very good.'

Hearing about all these clever people was about to ruin my Sunday, before it had even started.

The lift at The Strand was not working for some reason or other, so we had to lug Sometime up the stairs between us but I was glad to have him along. The emptiness of Sunday made me feel lonely. There were some pigeons strolling about on the platform. Jan got the tickets.

'How old is the teddy bear?'

The man behind the grill asked smiling, giving Jan a concession ticket for Sometime.

The train came in. It was so stained and dirty; you could hardly see out of the windows. It smelled as if it had been in the tunnel most of the time.

I sat at the window next to Sometime. We passed rows of derelict terraced houses. The people who lived there had been rehoused in the new tower blocks where they were isolated in steel and concrete, and they forgot who they were.

We got out at a small deserted station. The country was soft and green all around us in a washed-out blue sky. We walked up the road to the village. The houses began in rows of crooked red brick with tiny front gardens.

'I've lived in other houses.'

'I bet they were all posh.'

'Yes, they were.'

'I'd love to be rich.'

'Well, look at me now.'

'Then you shouldn't fight with your parents.'

'They shouldn't fight with me.'

'One day, you are going to have to go back home.'

'For what?'

'Because they are your parents.'

'I'm never going back.'

'You will.'

Jan took my hand and we walked up to the front door. A big man with braces opened the door.

'Jan!'

I thought he would hug Jan at least but instead, he said,

'How are you, my boy?'

'Papa, this is Nian.'

His father kissed me on both cheeks and once again on the other cheek.

'Who's your friend?'

He indicated to Sometime.

'Sometime.'

He did not know what to say to Sometime, so he asked us to come in. The house smelled of apples. Can you imagine living in a house that smells of apples? He took our coats and said we were to go to the back room. It was a sort of parlour. Jan dumped Sometime in a chair and flung himself down in front of the fire.

'I thought you might be a bit chilly, so I lit the fire today. Now you just make yourself at home and I'll get the tea on.'

'He's nice,' Jan said as his father went into the kitchen. The room looked onto the back garden. It was neat and well-tended with a long strip of lawn. The room was cluttered with photographs and odd souvenirs of places where they had spent their holidays. They did not seem sad, just unnecessary.

'You are looking fine, Jan.'

'I'm living with someone who cooks well.'

'You live with someone who can cook?'

His father was astonished. It was just as well he would never meet Geoff. He took me into the garden to see his roses. I liked flowers. I had my own garden once. Jan was playing with Marmalade, his father's large ginger cat. It reminded me of Kitty, the black and white kitten my mother had found outside the kitchen. She adored Kitty. She kept him in her room; together they watched television and did the crosswords. Kitty was not very good at crosswords and preferred to sit at the window with his tail swishing at the birds he longed to catch, so he bided his time and one day he escaped, like me. I had not thought about them in ages; I did not miss them. I loved them. I wished I could go home like Jan.

'Where did you meet, Jan?'

'We were both working in the theatre.'

'Jan is like his mother. She was a dancer in the theatre. Did he tell you? She loved the theatre, like Jan. Even when we married and after Jan was born, I know she missed it still. I worry for Jan. I would like him to study something. I wish I had Jan's mother to talk to him. She would know how to advise Jan, tell him what he should do with his life, maybe.'

'Jan is very lucky to have you,' was all I said.

After lunch, Jan's father suggested we go and watch telly while he washed up.

'We did not come to watch telly; we came to see you.'

Jan went and got his father's coat from the stand in the hall, helping his father into it.

'Come, we are going for a walk.'

Clouds had been gathering. They eddied across the sky, giants chasing each other. We walked up the lane alongside a field.

'Did you remember to bring sugar?'

Jan held out two sugar lumps to his father, who said,

'Since I have lived here, I have been going here for a walk every Sunday; there have always been horses in the field.'

We walked to where they were leaning over the gate.

'Go on, Jan. I'll be here next week.'

Jan held out his hand. The horses moved, heavy and patient, to take the sugar from him.

We wandered along the lane going in a wide circuitous route around the field, Jan hugging his father's arm close to him. We passed the horses on the way back. They were still there, still leaning over the gate. It would rain tonight. The air was sweet and I think then that day at least would always be England.

Chapter Seventeen

It began to warm up; the trees had suddenly become covered with bright green leaves. There was a flowering peach tree outside Luca's window. I broke off a few thin branches of the pale pink flowers. I felt Luca's reluctance to take the flowers I held out to him as he opened the door. Not wanting to offend me, he took them.

'This was kind of you. Thank you.'

He stood with me, unwilling to go back inside. The words when he spoke were like the dark notes drawn in ink.

'My wife always loved flowers. We had very little money and I thought they were an extravagance and begrudged her them. She was holding the flowers out to the soldiers when she was shot.'

He looked past me to the flowering tree.

'Now when I see such beauty, I know why my heart is beating and I am alive.'

He found an empty milk bottle for the tiny fragile flowers that would fade in a few hours, placing them next to the grimy kitchen window he never opened. Luca looked older; the basement he lived in was more untidy, emptier. He handed me my coffee and began to go through the clutter of music sheets.

'Would you like to learn some of the songs from my country?'

I was surprised. I had to practise complicated scales that were difficult for me and sing unmusical arias for ages; now he went over to the piano. I didn't want to sing. I wanted to listen to Luca play the piano; his interpretation of sound was so joyful.

'This is a folk song my father taught me. He was the musician in our family. He taught me to play the piano. Now I will teach you to sing this song from my country.'

He looked at me expectantly, waiting for my response. I struggled with the words because they were not in English. Luca patiently went over them one line at a time until I had mastered the song. We were alone in the ebbing silence when he had finished playing.

'I can only recapture them in music, my wife, my mother and father, my country.'

Worn and emptied by his loneliness, Luca had replaced my private tutor who had slipped out of my life without a ripple once I had gone to drama school. Now Luca was making me part of a strange picture, painting me into his life as he spoke of the people he loved.

I caught the bus back to Charing Cross going down to the river and walked across the pedestrian bridge, a barge, moving slowly in the fading light, lent enchantment to the end of the afternoon. I wished that I could cry, to prove that I, like Alice in Wonderland, was real.

I was sitting on the stepladder next to Sometime, watching the rain soak the drab garden and Jan's keep-off-the-grass sign when Courtly peered round the door.

'There I was humming *Over the Rainbow*, and there he was for the asking, darlings.'

'Jan!' Jan who had left us for tea in the green-panelled kitchen.

'Where have you been?'

'Out and about.'

'I'll bet.'

'You've become so crude.'

Gentle Jan with his dark hair and dark eyes was becoming distant from us. I could only say, 'Don't go.'

Jan began to scamper around the kitchen re-enacting the role of the white rabbit from the pantomime he had starred in. When he was a child star the audience and his mother adored him. I think that's why Jan likes working in the theatre even if being the call-boy is typecasting. The telly was on and Sandie Shaw was singing *Puppet on a String*. We all danced around the kitchen, me and Sometime, Courtly and Jan. Then

Jan stopped and danced with me and Courtly with Pravin, and we let Sometime sit this one out.

Soon after that, Jan moved back, bringing Robert with him. Geoff, it would seem, had been harbouring dreams of a ménage á trois.

Chapter Eighteen

Life at drama school had improved. We were to be taught for the first half of the new term by an outside director. Roy, who was about thirty, balding with sandy hair, had no time for Stanislavsky; his passion was producing and directing plays. But his contract meant we had to complete certain prescribed exercises. This involved remembering situations that we could recall to add authenticity to our acting. The first exercise was fear. I could not breathe. I made it to the cloakroom, pressing my knuckles into my mouth to stop my whimpering. Jemma came in and sat down on the floor next to me.

'Don't let them get to you. Just pretend, that's what I do.'

I caught a shattering sob.

'It's okay to cry.'

She hugged me reassuringly.

'When my mother died, I was sent to boarding school. I cried every day. I was nicknamed "sobbing Sally"; they were horrible. My mother always called me "Jemima Puddle Duck".'

'It suits you.'

'Not as a stage name.'

She stood up.

'You okay now?'

I stayed in the cloakroom, fearful of the trap that had been sprung.

Roy was producing a play for the amateur group he was involved with. Stagecraft was his thing, so he arranged for us to watch a rehearsal in progress. Roy was very enthusiastic and tended to bounce when he walked, using his hands in broad gestures to emphasise a point.

We treated this as a day out. The idea that we would learn anything never occurred to us; they were amateurs. Harvey, who was a wonderful mimic, copied Roy as he led the way across the common to the community hall Roy hired for the plays he produced.

There were lots of people milling about the urn with hot water for coffee and tea, and biscuits. They ignored us, lively and chatty, full of good humour and camaraderie. We were horribly out of place. These people had nothing to do with us. The play was, *The Inspector Calls*. Roy wanted us to learn how to make an entrance and exit on a stage as we watched other cast members. Abby was there. She was the maid. Shocked, Belle turned to us.

'What happened?' She was concerned.

'Wasn't she pregnant?'

Mila spoke carefully, not wanting other people to hear her.

'They asked her to leave because she has no talent.'

Jemma interjected abruptly, insistently stopping any further discussion.

I knew then that Jemma had helped Abby.

'Poor Abby, how horrible for her.'

Clea waved at Abby.

Abby ignored Clea, turning away from us.

The rehearsal was long, involving endless repetition, going over the same scenes until Roy was satisfied. We formed ourselves into a clique, drinking tea and eating their biscuits, bored with the play by the time we watched the run through.

Walking back across the common, I found no laughter in Harvey's antics. They did not negate something I could not comprehend, people content in shadows, happy in a world of make-believe.

For the last part of our training with Roy we were put into groups and worked on the first act of the plays he had chosen for us. It was just as well we had watched the rehearsal as he struggled to detach us from our emotions, directed us and expected us to learn the lines and not bump into the furniture.

I was given a part in a comedy. At last, I had someone else's words. I could fly.

Roy was waiting for me after our last rehearsal.

'Tell me what are you doing here?'

'I am learning to act.'

'You can do that already. You have a wonderful sense of timing, the hallmark of a fine actress.'

I felt as though I was looking into a dark well trying to see my reflection in the water below, afraid if I leaned over too far, I would drown. The only thing that stopped me was the structure and demands of this school.

'I have nowhere to go if I leave here.'

Roy said quite emphatically, 'They can't teach you. They can only harm you.'

So much for the roof over my head!

All the tutors watched our end-of-term productions. I made my entrances and exits on cue.

I was bright and funny. I was drowning.

Chapter Nineteen

There was a letter for me from New York with the First Day of Issue Stamp, a photograph of the Earth taken from space with the caption: "In the beginning…" and an airline ticket to Paris.

'Well, my dear, it seems Anton wishes to fuck you,' Courtly said when he had finished reading the letter. I smiled; it pleased me. Courtly also smiled. In everything we shared, lost as we were, there was a gentleness and honesty I was not to find again. Courtly leaped out of bed and began to make a massive breakfast. I sat on the stepladder with the kitchen full of steam and the smell of cooking. Courtly flounced off to get the eggs out of the pan. Not to be outdone, Jan flung the tea towel over his shoulder, vamping Courtly, who winked and blew him a kiss. I laughed and laughed, not because they were funny but because I loved them.

Anton phoned a few days later.

'Hello, Nian, do you know who this is?'

'Yes.'

Very much as an afterthought, I added,

'Thank you for the letter and air ticket.'

'That was a pleasure. Will you come to Paris?'

'Yes.'

'Thank you for your letters.'

I had written to him telling him about London because I had walked so much of it into me.

There were times when I thought I could only be because I lived here, so I wrote to him, sending fragments of captured moments.

'Your letters mean so much to me. You're so young, so free. Sometimes I long just to crawl into your arms and forget everything.'

I shut my eyes against the darkness in me.

'Promise you will come to Paris.'

'I promise.'

'A promise is a promise.'

I put the phone down. I was the only one there, me and Courtly. Courtly, who was whimpering somewhere in the house, he was being washed away like the rain that kept falling.

The rain still makes me think of Courtly, even when I don't mean to.

Chapter Twenty

I flew to Paris as planned over half term, leaving Sometime to look after Jan and Courtly.

He was waiting for me in the arrival hall. He smiled and took my arm.

'Did you have a good flight?'

He guided me to a real French taxi. We went to the hotel we were staying in. I looked out of the window.

'Do you like Paris?'

'Paris smells different but I like her.'

He walked over to me and carefully took Courtly's flowers from me. Courtly had walked with me to the station, stopping to buy flowers from Ma Tanner who was always there at the top of the stairs, bowing graciously as he handed them to me, making us strangers on the platform waiting for a train.

Somewhere far away, bells really did begin to ring. He drew the curtains; we were on the fourth floor, so I said,

'No, don't do that.'

'Well, then I must share you with Paris.'

I stood naked before him. When he kissed me it was like gathering the whole world into my arms and me into me. I found in my commitment to him part of the essence of me I would have lost but for the fact that, if only in this moment, we shared the fragile fabric of this time.

It was quiet; I lay with nothing but the indifferent intense awareness of my body. For the first time in my life, I could accept it because I had found it so pleasing. I was held by both the evening coming and this man I did not know, but whom I could reach across time and space.

Walking along the Boulevard de la Madeleine Paris was oddly quiet considering it was the going-home traffic.

'You're very thoughtful.'

He took my hand, turned my palm up and kissed it in the commitment of himself to me, eloquent now.

'Are you sleepy?'

'No.'

We walked and walked, climbing up the steep cobble streets to a church I saw in the distance. It was built drunkenly half way up the hill, soft brown against the skyline. I went up to the door, immediately dwarfed by it. It made me feel strange and out of place.

'It's a Catholic Church; would you like to go in?'

The door was not locked and I went into the long-ago smell of incense and the gloom of a strange church. On the side altars were candles. I bought one, kneeling for a long time in front of the candle, burning down with all those others. I wanted to be brave and when I knew more about the makings of me, I wanted to know I had done the hardest and the best and that I was a good soldier. I really was some kind of nut about being a good soldier. But then any compromise would have led to an irrevocable loss of a part of me and I was afraid of that.

'Do you believe in God?'

'Yes.'

'I envy you your faith.'

'Why?'

'Because I don't have any.'

We were quiet after that. I think we were both brooding about me lighting the candle. I was so aware of the newness of the smells and things that, when we walked past some woman, warm and strange, middle-aged, selling hot spicy pancakes on the street corner, I was enchanted. For once, I did not think about tomorrow. I was so wrapped up in the essence of now.

The room was hot when we got back. He turned on the fan; it whirled lazily over the bed. Outside in the dark, Paris was a blaze of lights.

'Would you like dinner now?'

'No, I want you to make love to me.'

'Now?'

I considered it without considering it at all.

'Yes.'

I wanted him within me. I responded to him as the sum total of everything I had come to be and I found it simple and complex. Making love, there was no way in which he could degrade me as he wished to do. It did not shock or even surprise me. I was only pleased to be able to tell him so easily that he could not shame me; there was nothing I would not allow or offer him, naked now, or a long way away when I learnt to understand. He cried out and I held him close with all my being.

When I woke in the morning, for the first time for as long as I can remember, I did not feel as though I had fallen into the sky. Instead, I saw Paris not yet awake, washed in the first light, luminous and pale yellow. I was awake when the birds started to sing and bring sound to the day. He turned over and touched my face with his fingertips.

'When you hold me, I feel as though you hold the whole world in your arms.'

I didn't answer, with his lips warm against my skin.

'You see, I know,' he said very softly into the hollow of my throat.

From across the Seine, Notre Dame, imposing, flocked by tourists looked almost white in the bright sunlight. I was going back to London. It was a hot very clear day and everything, and us, might as well have been painted on the brilliant blue sky. I was trying to remember everything as it happened.

'I don't know how to let go,' I said.

'Well, you must.'

'Yes.'

It cost me the fabric of sadness now and beyond.

'I am glad to have met you.'

I turned away from him. I longed to be in London, in her anonymous streets and hide myself, away from all the loneliness that did of course come. We went and sat at a pavement cafe, like tourists.

'You're very young; you have your whole life in front of you.'

'Yes,' I said because it all had so little meaning.

'You see, I'm married. My life is spoken for.'

I smiled then.

'I know.'

People kept walking past us. They were still doing that when he said,

'We are so nearly in love with each other.'

All I wanted was a little more time with him, and then I would have felt braver.

'I'm sorry if I have caused you any unhappiness. I did not mean to do that. I just wanted to be with you for whatever time there was.'

He went to the airport with me. I felt lost because he was so distant, then he kissed me indifferently, gently.

I caught the coach from the terminal with this great ache all over me, as though I were going to cry; only I could not. London with her thousands of tourists reached out from nowhere to nowhere. I didn't want to think about anything. I wanted to lie down and sleep; only I did not feel tired. Odd thoughts kept crowding in. I distorted already-distorted thoughts because I was afraid they, people, would find out something about me, something I didn't know myself. It was all so sad.

I was sitting on the stepladder in the kitchen holding Sometime, looking out at the backyard of the house next door and the tree that had not flowered yet, when a long time later Jan came bouncing in.

'Well, look who is back. Has he left you, the cad?'

'No, that was the agreement; we would only meet once.'

'Jesus! Girl. There are plenty of men, my dear. I should know.'

'Yes, but then I don't think we have the same taste in men at all.'

'We could, you know. I mean, I've fallen for straight boys. What a way to break your heart!'

He hung his arms up like a cross. I smiled because I thought it would be ungracious if I did not. Then Jan went off to work at the bistro. Holding Sometime in the lukewarm darkness, I began to whimper and then the sound overwhelmed me.

Chapter Twenty-One

The sun was shining on the sea. Jan had planned this trip to Brighton as a surprise. We walked past families, parents sitting in deckchairs, men in their shirtsleeves, their children's laughter, salty, untouchable. We sat down on the pebbly beach. Courtly sat on Jan's jacket because he was so thin; the stones would have hurt him. He rolled up his sleeves. His arms were marked with red lines and scars. He saw that I had seen them and grimaced.

I shivered.

'Are you cold?' Jan was concerned.

'I want to walk along the pier.'

Jan pulled me to my feet. I took Courtly's hand to help him up, sensing his reluctance to go anywhere. Music blared out from the different arcades on the pier. Courtly went and got us tickets for the ghost train. We crowded into the little car and screamed our way through the grimy dusty tunnels, holding onto each other and laughing at being scared by something so silly. Jan and Courtly went off into the arcades to play on the slot machines. I did not like being in those dark crowded rooms, so I wandered about the pier and bought Brighton rock.

Jan strolled along the pier to where I was sitting.

'Where is Courtly?'

'He's gone to Madam Nanine, the fortune-teller.'

Jan sat down on the bench next to me.

'Where's your jacket?'

'I gave it to Courtly. He was cold.'

We sat together eating the Brighton rock, waiting for Courtly to join us as the morning became afternoon. The wind blowing off the sea stirred us. Courtly should have come back ages ago.

'Shit.'

Jan stood up, looking around him anxiously.

'My wallet with all my money and the coach tickets are in my jacket.'

'I'm glad he has the money.'

I looked into the bleak sunshine.

I knew Courtly had gone to score, and the day would be lost to him.

Jan had some apples in his bag and we munched them while we decided what to do next. We wandered along the fun arcades along the seafront half looking for Courtly. Inside, the arcades were gloomy and almost empty, the sound of an organ-grinder echoing in the shadows. Jan looked ghostly in the neon lights. I was tired and hungry. I knew Jan was anxious. He didn't know what to do.

The lights along the front came on, beautiful old Victorian lamps, the wrought iron posts beginning to rust. We sat down wearily, leaning our backs against the railings lulled by the sound of the sea, the colour of the water darkening as the sky too darkened, becoming deep blue. I thought of Luca marooned as he was here in another country. I began to sing a folk song he had taught me, the haunting words mingling with the noise from the pier. Jan shut his eyes resting against me. I sang the strange beautiful song as if everyone could see Luca through me. I wanted Luca to escape his exile.

People stopped to listen, passing in slow motion, strangers wandering without purpose as the day faded unnoticed into night. Luca's music freed me. I knew something they could not. I was no longer invisible.

That was where Courtly found us. We managed to get the last coach to London. The beachfront disappeared as we drove into the narrow streets of Brighton. I looked back at the moon rising far out to sea, reflecting on the water; the stars were gone. I leaned over and kissed Jan.

'Thank you for a lovely day.'

Chapter Twenty-Two

The summer that had been sneaking up on us all the time, arrived.

It was very hot. Luca never opened the windows.

'Will you have coffee with me?'

He always asked me that with a slight bow in my direction. I stood awkwardly in the cluttered room.

'Sit.'

Luca smiled. It made him seem younger. I looked around for somewhere to sit. The only place was a small sofa that was strewn with sheets of music. I gathered them up, putting them into a pile.

'We must begin something new. It is time for you to extend your range.'

'I like your songs. I sang them on the seafront at Brighton. People thought I was a busker.'

'You sang the beautiful songs from my country like a beggar .Why?'

Luca was shocked, disapproving.

'I didn't want you to be invisible.'

Luca turned to me with an expression of startled anguish.

'You told me that was why you wanted to sing, to be visible. I could understand that.'

We were both afraid, now conscious of each other, unable to meet across the divide between us – guilt. Luca stepped forward and made the sign of the cross on my forehead.

'My mother never forgot her Catholic roots. For her I bless you, because I fled my country. I am lost to her now.'

I sat very still, looking at the black notes on the white paper. I could not read music; to me, music had no words. I needed to confess to Luca.

'Since their accident, my parents only had me.'

The radio was off. There were no other voices.

'It seems that we have both abandoned our families to save ourselves.'

I turned away from what Luca had said. Beyond the basement window and the iron stairs was the overgrown garden and the peach tree with fruit stung and rotting on the branches. Luca spoke in the silence that had engulfed us.

'Sometimes I think I would rather have died than live in exile.'

'Yes,' I said because I understood.

Luca lifted his hands in an odd gesture of supplication.

'I am sorry. Despair is a terrible thing.'

He walked past me to the piano and began to play, the haunting liquid notes enveloping us there so that there was no separation. That afternoon, I practised scales. I did not sing anything. Luca got up at the end of the lesson and began looking for his book where he kept a record of the lessons he gave.

'You will come again on Thursday?'

Most of the pages were empty. Luca did not have many students. I could not come back here. More and more I wanted to retreat into darkness. Luca's music had become a burden. It contained the secret language that would unlock my heart and I was not brave enough. He got up courteously to see me out, the sound of the traffic making the room mean and small. As I went up the stairs leading into the neglected garden Luca turned on the radio. It made me so sad.

Chapter Twenty-Three

I had another role, a victim of an abusive relationship. I envied Dee. She had a wonderful part, a neurotic woman that appealed to me; my private tutor had said I was lucky I had a touch of madness and it was all going to waste. I was careful to avoid my chaotic feelings, they held me hostage. Jesse, who was cast as the abusive husband, a super-macho male part, was incapable of anger or unkindness. I gave up the pretence of using props to escape the confrontation demanded by the script. We were an odd pair as I put my arms around gentle doomed Jesse, without understanding; this was a gift of learning.

As the term progressed new classes were added. Debby, one of the tutors, now took us for speech lessons. Once again, we were asked to interpret various tracts using our own words. It was intimidating. We were all fearful of being wrong. Then one afternoon, we could each choose a poem to read out aloud.

Vincent chose *Fern Hill*, speaking the words of Dylan Thomas with such passion and clarity.

Did they know then we were listening to something so magical that even now I hold my breath? If he never achieved anything, it did not matter. That afternoon, he was great.

I had to walk from the station to the house. It had cooled down. The sun was dropping away behind the houses and shining through the trees with the leaves caught in the trembling light, a picture breaking into fragments. Everything was familiar but I didn't know where I was. I could not remember where I lived. I was lost in a silence I did not understand.

The television was on. I slowly focused on hearing, trying to decipher the words.

'Are you alright?'

Courtly was sitting on the floor in the semi-dark room.

'There's some tea for you. I found you in the street.'

I drank my tea slowly. I was glad it was dark and Courtly was here.

'I didn't know where I was.'

Courtly wasn't really listening. He was agitated.

'Nian, do you have any money?'

'Not much.'

'How much do you have?'

'About five pounds.'

'Can I borrow it? I'll let you have it back.'

'No, you can have it. It's okay.'

'I need it now.'

'Can't you stay? You do live here.'

He smiled.

'I'd forgotten that.'

'Well, keep it in mind.'

He didn't answer.

Courtly put his mug down and began to weep, hugging his arms around his knees. I knelt beside him, holding his stiff body.

'Don't cry. It will be alright. It will be alright.'

'It won't be alright, Nian, ever.'

I held him until he stopped crying. Then I got him the money.

Courtly put his arms around me. When he kissed me, I tasted the salt of all those tears.

'You mustn't cry,' he said.

Chapter Twenty-Four

Roy was replaced by Howard for the last quarter. Roy had been introduced to us with some fanfare as an innovative young producer. Howard was just there, out of place in the noisy canteen, tall, grey-haired and about sixty. To us, that meant he was older than God. We had no idea who he was. He was so unassuming that when he introduced himself, we did not know how to respond. The next surprise was there would be no class. Instead as part of our training, the school had made a block booking to see the Russian entry to the international theatre festival. The news was greeted with both disbelief and then excitement. I was left out. I felt nothing.

I have often wondered if it was because the play was produced by a different culture in another language. It was so absorbing, funny and endearing. Before the curtain came down an old man, Firs, locked into the house by accident because the family he had served have forgotten him, remarked that he might never have lived, as he listened to the sound of the cherry orchard being chopped down. I wept pure tears without grief. I understood at last the elusive magic.

Howard wanted to know what audition pieces we had chosen. One was always set by the school. The other was what we chose. I was surprised at how dark and complicated they were. Howard asked us politely why we had chosen the dramatic works we had, knowing our future could depend on these choices, listening respectfully to the answers, but to some of my group, it made them hostile and defensive.

As an exercise we had to go through our audition pieces in front of the class. Being subjected to the scrutiny of our peers was terrifying. Jemma, who was last, burst into tears when she had finished. Howard said diffidently,

'It is something you need to learn, to hold your own against members of the cast, the audience, the dead eye of the camera.'

We were glad to be the only ones in the canteen taking comfort from the familiar room.

'It is very important to consider why you want to be an actor or actress. It is not only a huge commitment but also guarantees heartache and disappointment.'

Howard had joined us in the canteen, unobtrusively standing at the urn with his coffee.

'Talent is not enough; luck helps. A lot of your time will be spent waiting for the next audition. It is often a very lonely profession. The theatre can demand too much.'

He paused as though expecting us to reply.

'You are all so young.' He was smiling. It changed him.

'Believe me when I say you can both be productive and happy and not be in this profession.'

I had never thought of being productive or happy.

We were in the auditorium of one of the most famous theatres in world. Just being there made us speak in hushed tones. Howard, we realised, must know important people to allow us this privilege. We had chosen excerpts from our favourite plays to perform on this stage alone, not in front of our group. Howard had warned us some of the cast from the play might look in but not to let this disturb us, to remember we were in command of the stage and the auditorium.

'Good actors should always be curious,'

Howard remarked ruefully. But we didn't understand.

We were ushered into a rehearsal room where we waited nervously to be called. I was the last one. The pubs had just opened, so my group swarmed out chattering and laughing, birds flying away from the place that had held them captive.

The stage and the auditorium were familiar to me. I had worked in a theatre with Jan and Pravin, Stan had been there to keep us safe.

'What have you chosen?'

Howard's question was lost in the darkness.

I have chosen Dido Morgan's monologue on love from *The Marching Song* by John Whiting.

Calmness came over me as though I was confessing and would be forgiven.

As I began, the door to the auditorium opened as someone slipped in.

When I heard this play on the radio, listening to Dido was as though I had been blind and was now able to see. Now, standing here, I could make her manifest on an empty stage; there were no more words. I remained encapsulated in this moment.

'You are magically talented. Do you know that?'

I could not see who was speaking. Then I recognised his voice.

It was dark outside. Looking up at the moon shinning far beyond the black branches of the trees, I was filled with such wonder that it spilled into the sky with everything touched by my presence. I had a great talent, one I had not expected or wanted. It had been seen and recognised. Being brave did not seem so pointless. I, the good soldier, had been blessed.

On Monday, we waited expectantly for Howard to appear, secretly wanting him to validate our experience at the theatre. At midday, one of our tutors informed us that Howard had been called away and that another tutor would take our afternoon class. There was some discussion about Howard's sudden disappearance, but he was incidental. He did not have the gravitas of the school; his memory faded and frayed, but for me remained.

The feeling that I had been unmasked as an imposter made me more and more isolated from my group, locked in and fearful. Classes were now sporadic as the focus was on the third-year students. Greg, the music teacher, wanted us to have something to show for the end of the year. We were to compose a song. My life was strung out by meaningless actions using me up. I was hanging by a thread. I sang my song. There was a fluttering sound like birds beating their wings uselessly against the window; applause.

When I was not at school, the empty house became oppressive, unbearable. I began banging my head against the wall, wailing. That frightened me. I found some pills Courtly left lying about and I lay down, empty of all feeling.

'Jesus! Girl!'

Jan was sitting on the floor next to my bed with Sometime.

'You really freaked me out.'

'Why?'

'Why she says? You try living with someone who spends hours and hours on her bed not speaking, just looking up at the ceiling.'

'I was listening to my heartbeat.'

'And is it still beating?'

'Yes.'

'Well, get you!'

Jan picked up Sometime, holding him against his face so I could not see his expression. Jan stayed like that until I finally got up. I had found a way out. With a bit of luck I would be able to get back to the time I knew nothing about.

Chapter Twenty-Five

Then Courtly died. We were in the kitchen when there was a knock at the door. I went down to see who was there. He asked me if I knew a Charles Grant of this address. He, in his smart blue uniform, was standing out on the deserted pavement. The young constable with the stripes on his jacket was very kind; he needed the address of Courtly's parents. They were his next of kin.

'Who is there?'

Jan had come to the top of the stairs.

I had closed the front door without thinking.

'The fuzz.'

'What do they want?'

I didn't answer. Courtly kept his parents' address in his copy of *Winnie the Pooh*. It was written on the back of a photograph of him with his family. Robert took the joint away from Jan and threw it down the toilet; Jan began to wave his arms around to dispel the smoke and tossed all the hash into the teapot.

'Courtly is dead.'

I went back downstairs. I watched the police car drive away, trying to imagine a world without Courtly. It was Sunday afternoon with the sun gentle yellow on everything. I knew it would not get dark for ages. I walked out of the house and into the street, walking that time and all that grief into me.

The house was empty when I got back. I went and watched the telly, the Sunday movie, the Late Night line-up and the epilogue. I turned the telly off, made some tea, and sat on the stepladder, trying, like most people do, to hold Courtly close to me.

I was wanted for an interview. I was not surprised. At the beginning of that week, we were to be to be judged by the improvisation we had been working on. We had, as a group, to imagine we were alone in a room with an imaginary mirror. Now we would be alone on the stage. I was frozen, unable to express anything, terrified that when I looked in the imaginary mirror, I would not be there. I stood on the empty stage in front of them for as long as I could bear it. Then I crumbled to my knees, putting my hands over my ears, shutting my eyes and curling into a ball. At last, I had shown who I was and I knew I was doomed.

My whole class shied away from me for the rest of that agonising day. The holy trinity was waiting for me, the three most important tutors; no one else's opinion counted. Seated behind the long table, there they were, ready to withdraw the Word of God. I listened to them going on about my not being able to cope with the training I was getting. They had looked for and seen no improvement. I had failed to develop. They were very disappointed in me. Of course, they would have to take some responsibility because at my audition they had believed I had shown potential.

'It is just that you have no talent as an actress.'

I stood up, before I could close the door, Sven, the old movement instructor, who had given up his whole life to teaching said, 'I believe you have great ability. It just needs to be released.'

It made me want to weep. Thank God, that part of my self-therapy was over. The school, as I walked away from it, became impenetrable. The indelible lines that shaped me would remain, but I had lost them, my group, on that terrifyingly empty day.

We had a wake for Courtly. Pravin cooked a meal for us to keep us from going anywhere, but he need not have bothered. We had nowhere to go.

'What will you do for the summer?'

I was helping Pravin with the vegetables.

'I thought I would go to India to see if I can find some of my family. It might be difficult with a name like Patel.'

Pravin was thoughtful just thinking about it.

'I would love to go to India.'

'Is that because of *The Beatles*?'

'No, it's because of you.'

Pravin smiled then.

This morning he had put candles next to the statue of Ganesh. Pravin knew about death. He had lost both his mother and his father. Now there was the little alter with candles and incense burning. They were for Ganesh; we were immortal. I opened the back door that led out into the garden. Jan threw some crusts out for birds. Robert was sitting on the lawn reading the Sunday papers. We joined him, sitting next to Jan's "Keep off the Grass" sign. Robert handed me *The News of The World*. He kept *The Observer* to re-affirm his prejudices. Hidden amongst the small print and bits of news was a picture of Courtly. He looked so pure and unused; I almost did not recognise him. Jan sitting next to me was reading over my shoulder.

"Charles Edward Grant aged nineteen was found dead of a suspected drug overdose on Hampstead Heath".

Jan did not look up from the photograph as he said, 'Trust Courtly to make a splash. The Queen of the Nile could not have done better.' Then we laughed.

I was glad of that day. We had so little to offer. Courtly was entitled to our grief, what there was of it in that sad awkward lunch.

Chapter Twenty-Six

Roy phoned out of the blue. Knowing that my brilliant career had disappeared, I should have been doing something to justify my existence but I did not do anything other than try and keep the fear that stalked me at bay. Without Courtly, the phone had not rung in ages.

'Nina?'

'Yes.'

'I was told that you left.'

'Not because I wanted to.'

'But it's a good thing. Now you can use all that energy in a positive way.'

All that energy had turned into terror.

'I know of a summer company. They will be holding auditions. You could try out for them.

'Remember what I said? You don't need a drama school. You have so much talent.'

It was as though I was under ether. Courtly was dead and here I was planning my future, the one I did not want, the one Courtly would never have.

I went to the audition Roy told me about. I had to honour his generosity. He could have offered me a place in his amateur group and that would have done me in. I left early to escape the house, taking the tube to Regent's Park. I wandered to the water's edge, past the flowers wilting in the heat. I was empty of everything, even sound, as I tried to find some caring that was gentle and not angry in me. I needed the knowledge of grief to be free as I turned to stone.

There were ducks at the edge of the water; there had been ducks on the pond near my grandmother's house. I did not see my parents for over two years after the accident in America. They had been in hospital for a long time because they both needed specialist and ongoing treatment and rehabilitation. The dreadful days when they were in intensive care faded. My father arranged for me to spend my school holidays with my grandmother; she was my bulwark against the fear that my parents had abandoned me. My father wrote sporadic dutiful letters giving an account of their lives, mostly just about the food and the nurses and then the views from the apartment they had rented but nothing about them. My mother never wrote. She had always sent postcards on which she drew funny faces and wrote into the bubbles she drew, but she sent none from America.

I spent a lot of time during the school holidays hunting for antiques with my grandmother, collecting china plates. I liked them and began to learn about china. My grandmother was proud of my knowledge and interest. She saw me now as less of the burden and more of a companion. We would spend weekends searching for bargains. In the evening, we played cards and listened to the radio, content in each other's company.

When I was called into the office by the headmistress, I had expected news from my parents, not to be told that my grandmother was dead.

My father flew out for the funeral. My grandmother was well known in her village, so there was quite a turnout. Because she was old, not many tears were shed. My grandmother had always remained the same, stern and upright, imposing order and discipline; she had been the one constant in my life, and standing here, she still was.

The elderly people who filled the church sang lustily, enjoying the hymns. My father did not sing. He was burying his mother. At the end of the service, we stayed back. My father walked up to the casket and took a rose from the floral arrangement. He handed it to me in a strangely gracious gesture. I took it from him and kissed it, laying the single rose on the casket and said goodbye to my beloved grandmother. My father stood silent in his grief, unwilling to leave. I wanted to comfort him, to say something but he was a stranger. He had come back an old man with greying hair and walked with cane and now wore glasses.

He also carried a bitterness within him that would pervade my life.

I shut my eyes. I opened them again because the thought that had been formulating suddenly became very clear. I wanted to go home.

After my grandmother's death, my parents had returned. I had not seen my mother since the accident. My mother was standing at the window. She turned as I came in. I screamed, horrified. My effervescent beautiful mother looked at me with one eye frozen, blind, set down in its socket.

Her face contorted into an expression of hatred; the damage was done. My mother tried to commit suicide that night. My father found her in the morning. She had taken an overdose of the antidepressants she had been given in America. I was left numb with grief and terror, alone in the house, waiting to be told my mother had died, knowing that it would be my fault. I knew saying I was sorry would never be enough. I did not have the words to put it right.

Chapter Twenty-Seven

I was at the wrong end of Oxford Street on my way to the audition when I saw Roy leaning out of the window of a taxi.

'Hello, my comedienne. Where are you going?'

'To the audition. I'm going to be famous.'

Roy laughed, suddenly young, away from his youth theatre.

'Good luck.'

I had not planned to be an actress. Now I would cease to exist if the people I was going to see this afternoon did not recognise I was talented.

I arrived there just about on time. It was such a dilapidated building that I bet they just rented it for the summer. There was another girl there. She had long, golden hair and big eyes; in fact, she looked like an actress. They had a creepy receptionist who was busy typing we-don't-want-you letters and chatting to her boyfriend. She took pity on me.

'They are running late. You might as well look at the magazines while you wait.'

I picked one up. It was full of glossy pictures of Vietnam War soldiers and dead people. The blonde girl came out; nothing in her demeanour had changed. She would just have to wait in the wings until her self-belief ran out.

Thomas, a final year student at drama school, came in. He was a real prick, but he had made it in just about every department I could think of, and most of my class.

'Hello!'

He could hardly believe I occupied the same space he did.

'I didn't expect to see you here. What have you been doing since you left?'

'Nothing.'

My disgrace, it seemed, was public knowledge.

'We have just done a very modern production of *Waiting for Godot*.

'Well, you're in the right place.'

Thomas just managed to stop himself from scowling. He did not know what I was talking about. They, my ex tutors were planning a brilliant future for Thomas. He was their idea of greatness. Godot would be waiting forever; they deserved each other.

'How are they?'

Thomas was above answering irrelevant questions, so he asked one instead.

'Are you also going to audition?'

I don't know what the hell he thought I was doing besides looking at these shitty magazines.

'You can go through.'

I got up.

'Good luck.'

I went into this large almost empty room. It had high windows and thick green carpeting, and it was dingy in there.

'Hello, sit down,' one of them spoke.

I sat in this chair facing them. They sat quite a long way away from me. If I bumped into them a day later, I would not have recognised them.

'You are?'

'Nina.'

'Of *The Seagull*?'

'Yes.'

'Do you understand her obsession?'

'Sometimes.'

'That should prove useful.'

'Have you worked in the theatre before?'

'Yes.'

'Oh, what did you do?'

'I worked backstage on the lighting board.'

One of them laughed.

'In your letter, you said you did not finish drama school. Why not?'

'I left?'

'We usually prefer those who completed their course.'

I was humbled.

'What do you hope to get out of the theatre?'

'Nothing.'

'That's interesting.'

'What do you think you have to offer us that would make us want to accept you?'

I could not see them properly in the funny room that reminded me of a cage. I had no answer for that.

'Are you a lesbian?'

'No.'

'Do you always use your femininity to dominate other people?'

'Don't you want to hear my audition pieces?'

'Yes, what did you prepare?'

'Nina from *The Seagull* and Iris from *Rattle for a Simple Man*.'

'That is an interesting choice.'

'Do you like Chekhov?'

'Yes.'

'Why?'

'He says funny things that are sad.'

'Are you going to make us laugh?'

'Do you find sad things funny?'

There was an awkward silence.

'Tell us, Nina, do you have the madness of the seagull?'

'Yes.'

'Are you an adequate person?'

'No.'

'Do you consider your first duty as an actress is to the author?'

'Yes.'

'How far are you prepared to go in order interpret the intention of the writer?'

'Are you passionate?'

'Would you fuck other members of the cast?'

I got up and went to the door.

'Where are you going?'

'Your little bird is flying away.'

'Wait.'

One of them got up from behind the table. I went through the reception and was walking down the stairs when he called down the stairwell. I looked up and saw him properly for the first time, his expression a blank mask. I knew then I would never audition again. My mantra no longer sustained me, so I began my endless tumble into the dark with nothing to catch me.

'We haven't made a decision yet.'

I was free. I reached the door that led out into the street.

'What's your phone number?' he called out, shocked.

'Don't call me. I'll call you.'

I did not look back. I stopped in Soho to buy flowers from the barrow men. As I passed under the street lights, holding the bright yellow daffodils on a summer evening in London, I filled her streets.

Chapter Twenty-Eight

There was a letter lying in wait for me when I got back. Pravin came into the kitchen.

'Did I tell you? I applied to Leeds University and I have been accepted.'

'That's good.'

What good this would do for him or the novel we were all in, I didn't know.

'Can we interrupt or are you having a mothers meeting?'

Robert and Jan were standing in the doorway.

'I'm going to university, to Leeds,' Pravin said shyly.

'Oh darling, why am I always the last to know?'

Robert exclaimed, winking at Jan.

'Are you going to be on campus?'

Robert went on archly, breaking the word up into syllables.

'What are you going to do at university?'

Jan had come into the kitchen.

'I'm reading English. I start at the end of September.'

'Are you going to live in Leeds?'

Jan was interested now.

'Yes, all students live in halls for the first year.'

'So you are going to be a proper student?'

'Yes.'

'Clever girl!'

It was perfunctory, Jan was busy looking for money to put in the meter, not at Pravin.

'My family would not have believed that I would be going to university.'

'Well, look at you now,' I said expansively. 'Your parents must be very proud.'

I could see Pravin's eyes twinkling behind his small round glasses. I thought it was because he was smiling, but it wasn't. It was because of his tears.

Time hung like a dead weight. Robert and Jan had gone out. I listened to Pravin moving about in his room. It was the only sound in the house, a soft intermittent oddly polite sound as if Pravin were afraid of making a noise. My room was cluttered with Courtly's things. Even now, I do not want possessions; they make me feel defeated. I sat on the unmade bed. The cloth of the sheet was rough and slightly damp. My whole body began to ache. I kept smoothing the sheets carefully with my hands, emptying myself into that touch.

Courtly's mother had gone alone to see him buried.

'No flowers, family only by request.'

This brown paper parcel from the morgue or something had arrived through the post. I got up and opened it. Courtly's clothes had been returned, his pink shirt, blue jeans, his shoes and socks and the silver wrist chain he always wore. I went into the kitchen to throw the wrapping in the bin; the letter on the table was addressed to me in green ink. Only my father used green ink; it was one of his affectations. The letter began. "Your mother..."

I had written to my parents to ask if I could come back for the summer holidays.

"My mother" in green ink and carefully formed words could not get over the injustice of the accident, it had left her scarred and ruined her life. I already knew that there was no justice unless you were a member of the Mafia, and my mother lacked the peace of God. Bitter and almost defeated, my father wrote, "Your mother has suffered enough without you putting her through your selfish unkind disappearance". My mother, who cried alone.

"For my part, I find your behaviour towards both your mother and me quite unacceptable".

I wanted to tear the letter into tiny pieces so I would never read it again, but I did not. I folded it up neatly, afraid to do anything else. I could not go home. It would be utterly pointless. Even now, I can recall the empty desolation as I put my face against Sometime's soft fur but his arms were locked, stiff and rigid at his sides.

Chapter Twenty-Nine

Jan was working long hours at the local bistro. He was saving to go on holiday with Robert. Robert wanted to go to art galleries in Italy. His discounted middle-class parents would pay for this while Jan was making salads, chopping vegetables and washing down the kitchen floors. That was lust for you. Jan came into my room and sat on the bed next to me.

'Is this what came in the post?'

He indicated to the clothes that I had left lying on the floor.

'I suppose we could send them to the YMCA.'

'Why? The YMCA isn't for the homeless.'

Jan got up. I really depressed him.

'You have them,' I said.

He hesitated.

'Robert rather fancies the leather jacket.'

'Does Robert also fancy necrophilia?'

'What?'

'Robert is not screwing Courtly now that he is dead. If he wants a two-hundred quid jacket, he can hustle for it.'

'What's the matter?' Jan was defensive.

'I'm going to give all Courtly's things, everything to the Salvation Army. Maybe it will buy him a place in Heaven.'

The next day, Jan took Courtney's wrist chain and made it smaller for me to wear.

'You're going to have it.'

He put the chain on my wrist.

'It looks nice.'

Jan was uncertain and out of his depth and I wished he could just have been as sad as I was for losing Courtly, because then he would not have been so puzzled or so forsaken. It was raining. It went on falling and falling over all the crooked houses as far as I could see.

Jan had to get his passport renewed before going on holiday to Italy with Robert. Robert was busy moulding Jan in his own image as I tried to snatch Jan back and keep him safe.

'I hope Robert keeps his eyes on artworks and not the real thing,' I mentioned as the train slowed. It was smothering hot on the tube. Jan got up; it was our station.

'But that is just what he wants as sure as God made little apples.'

'What? Works of art?' I was scornful.

'No.'

Jan widened his eyes in mock horror, 'The real thing, little apples!'

We were laughing as we raced each other up the tube steps out into the sunny street like little blind and deaf moles.

We were having tea at Lion's Corner House when grief seemed to walk in the door as though it had been following us all over London. Jan put his hands over his face to hide his tears.

'Courtly knew he was going to die; the fortune-teller on the Brighton Pier told him.'

Anguished, Jan looked up at me.

'He knew. Courtly knew.'

'What did she say?'

'She saw Courtly in a park.'

'I could imagine that,' I said gently, 'and I'm not clairvoyant.'

'Except that Courtly was dead.'

Chapter Thirty

I went out into the derelict garden when we got back from the Embassy, walking over the thin grass in the hot tepid afternoon. Everyone would be leaving soon and I could not bear to be here with Robert's friends, whom he called Abel and Mabel. When they arrived from the good old US of A, Abel and Mabel had decided to come to swinging London and be part of the scene; strangers would be living here while everyone else went away.

I looked back at the house, the sun shining on the windows, making it dark so you could not see inside. I could not spend the summer here and that would save me. Family is everything. It was like an echo. I remembered Luca saying that. My mother had a sister, Emily, in Canada and I would go to her.

I went up the West End and drifted into the plush interior of Pan Am and asked the girl behind the desk about flights to Canada. They were all hugely expensive. I kept asking if they had any cheaper flights like the bucket shops I had heard about. She was adamant against my insistence that there had to be a cheaper way to get to Canada. When I went out onto the hot pavement, he was standing in front of me. He had a funny beige suit and a waistcoat.

'I was standing behind you at the Pan Am counter. If you want a cheap flight to Canada, phone this number and mention my name.'

The next day, I phoned the number on the card. The person who answered after some hesitation, gave me an address where to bring the money. I withdrew the money and went on an endless bus ride to a basement with desks and people who took the money and issued me with a ticket. I was on my way to Toronto.

On the way back, sitting upstairs in the front of the bus, I saw Jemma walking on the pavement. Without thinking, I rang the bell, hopped off and ran back down the street. Jemma squinted at me. She needed glasses but refused to wear them.

'What are you doing here?'

'I have just bought a ticket to Canada. I am going to visit my aunt.'

'My only aunt married a rapist.'

She took my arm as though consoling me.

'I thought everyone knew about my sad childhood.'

'Do you live near here?'

Jemma looked around with distaste. It was an awful place with rundown terrace houses, broken front gates and neglected rubbish.

'No, Clea lives near here.'

'Clea of a thousand nights,' I said, because that was how I thought of her.

'Clea is now working as a Bunny Girl. She makes loads of bread. Jake pimps her out because men fancy her.'

I hoped that Clea would fly up onto a billboard like a dark moth and become famous.

It was beginning to rain and we took shelter in the shell of a bombed-out church.

Jemma went on matter-of-factly.

Clea was pregnant, once they found out she had to leave school. That meant she lost her grant money. She hid it as long as possible. Without the grant she had nothing.

'Will the baby be adopted?'

Jemma said without expression, 'Clea would never have given her child up.'

She looked into the distance as though trying to fathom something.

'Jake got done for dealing, so Clea was living alone in some grotty room. I went round to see if she was alright. Clea was in terrible pain and bleeding.' Remembering, Jemma gave a small shudder.

'I had to find a phone box that was not vandalised. It was so horrible. I was afraid to go back but this woman began knocking on the glass. There was so much blood; I thought she was dead. Then I saw the baby. It was so small,' Jemma said in a whisper.

'It was almost here.'

She looked away, the rain wetting her face.

'Before the ambulance arrived Clea gave me the silver and brass bells she always wore, in case she died.'

I put my arms round her and whispered so only she could hear.

'I'm sorry.'

I held her close for a moment. I wanted everything to be different. I wanted the great and the good to lead us to the path of righteousness.

They were all assembled in the kitchen when I got back to say goodbye to Pravin, who looked like a stranger in his in suit.

'Is that what you are taking?'

Jan indicated to the straw valise.'

'Yes, it was my mother's.'

'It looks like something left over from the Raj.'

Pravin flinched.

'I have the address of a relative of my father. I hope he is still in the same place. It is a long way to go. I have not flown before.'

Pravin stood undecided in the kitchen, reluctant to leave.

Jan took the woollen hat Sometime was wearing and put it on Pravin's head.

'Now you look like a writer in search of a story.'

Sometime did not need us to invent a life for him. He had become part of our lives and had nothing to say.

Chapter Thirty-One

Over the weekend, Robert had taken the Christmas lights down and painted the ceiling white again. The last vestige of Courtly was gone.

I had forgotten how to sleep and joined Jan in the kitchen when he came back from his late-night stint at the bistro.

'Would you like some tea?'

'May as well.'

I sat on the stepladder as Jan filled the kettle. It sounded really loud.

'If Robert was human, that would wake him.'

Jan hunched over the kettle with a small shiver.

'Robert is into a really bad scene.'

He wanted me to understand something that was important to him.

'Robert needs to be recognised as a great artist. It's the only value he places on his life.'

'And he isn't a great artist?'

I was scornful. I hated his concern for Robert. It was a trap. By dying, Courtly had achieved fifteen minutes of fame, or was it fifteen seconds? That was what Robert aspired to.

'I believe in him. No matter what, I'll still be here.'

'Why?'

Jan gave me a funny little smile.

'I hoped you just lusted after his beautiful body.'

'I do,' Jan sighed.

'I wish I could marry you.'

'And we would live happily ever after,'

I finished for him.

'My mother died before Christmas,'

Jan was forlorn.

'She had been ill for a long time but she did not want anyone to know.

Jan paused regretfully, remembering.

'For the curtain call I would fly up into the gantry. There was always a lot of applause.' Jan handed me my tea. 'I hoped that if I flew high enough, I would find my mother in the light.'

I took the mug from him.

'Ta'

'Anytime, love.'

I smiled.

'My dad sends you his regards. He asked why you had not come down with me this time. He sent you some apples, but I forgot them. I'm sorry.'

'That's okay. I'll bring you back something from Canada.'

'Who is going to look after old Sometime while we are all away?' Jan asked.

'He is going to look after the house for us.'

'You do that,' Jan said, lifting Sometime up and kissing him. Jan stayed like that with his face next to Sometime's blind eyes.

'One day, it is going to be just Sometime and me. You won't stay; others will come and go. So I have to fly.'

'Don't fly too high,' I said gently.

Jan, with his dark eyes, looked back at me. He had become essential; he would forever be part of the mystery of me.

We stayed up all night, dipping stale currant bread into our tea while Jan talked about his mother and his time as a child star. He had loved being on stage. His mother had always been there. Then she died. That ended his career; without her, it was pointless. I opened the window. The air smelled sweet of the long, long summer to come as I gathered that morning into me.

The flowering cherry tree that belonged next door came into bloom and I was in an empty house. Robert had gone, taking Jan and leaving the remnants of his hostility. I took the newspaper cutting with the photograph of Courtly off the wall, holding it crumpled in my hand and not knowing what to do with it. I went into the kitchen, found some matches and burnt it, ashes to ashes. Sound was retreating from whatever was left. I think I would have fallen back down the tunnel that was in me if I had not known that I would fly to Canada. I did not think what would happen after that. I just let go. I kissed Sometime goodbye and before the house sucked all the breath from my body, I ran from it.

Chapter Thirty-Two

I had arranged to spend the night before I flew to Canada with Jemma. I got there late because Jemma was working in a pub till closing time. She was living in a flat that inside looked like a window display of Habitat.

Jemma saw my surprise and laughed.

'Jerry is a pilot so everything has a purpose and everything has to be in the right place. So he ordered a catalogue house.'

'How did you come to live here?'

'Jerry's wife walked out on him, leaving him without clean white shirts he needed for work. He advertised for home help. I know how to wash and iron, now I am his layover lay.'

I felt awkward, an intruder in this loveless tryst.

'It's just sex,' Jemma said dismissively.

Small, dumpy Jemma with her pale freckled face was not beautiful. That was the currency of the day, I wondered if that was why Jemma was so compliant. Intimidated by the regimented order of the flat, we retreated to Jemma's small untidy room.

'Are you a virgin?' Jemma asked abruptly with a sort of aggressive curiosity.

'No.'

'Really?'

She squinted at me making her slightly comical.

'Did you love him?'

"When you hold me, I feel as though you hold the whole world in your arms". Anton had said that. It reverberated in my soul. That was my only understanding of love.

'Was he married?'

'Yes.'

'That's a really bad scene.'

She was sitting at the dresser facing the mirror.

'My father remarried and I inherited Cedric. A fourteen-year-old liar, thief and chronic wanker who was always trying to persuade me to hold his dick.'

Jemma rolled her eyes in mock horror making me laugh.

'When I complained, my stepmother went mad as though I had defiled her precious son.'

She began to brush her hair, concentrating on each stroke.

'My father could not face losing another wife, so I was sent to live with my aunt in Wales.'

'With the rapist?'

I was not being glib. I wanted her to know I had listened.

'Yes, that's the one.'

She watched me in the mirror.

'My aunt went to church every Sunday, leaving me alone with him.'

Before I could say anything, she turned back to me.

'He thought incest was best.'

'What did you do?'

I wanted her to know I cared.

'I told them how much money they had to give me or I would go to the police. I took the coach to London and found work as an au pair, working for Emelina who was Spanish and divorced with two little girls.'

'Once I was house-trained, Emelina told me that she would be away for the weekend. The children's father was coming over from Spain. She refused to see him when he visited the children. Amado made love to me that weekend. He was so gentle and patient. When I told him about my uncle, he said that he would kill him. He enjoyed being with his children. We played games, pretending that we were on a desert island, it was such fun. He used to call me his little treasure.'

Jemma smiled at herself in the mirror reaffirming the memory.

'Then Emelina realised what was happening and threw me out.'

She put the brush down and turned to me.

'I phoned Amado, I had nowhere to go.'

She gave a small involuntary shudder.

'I trusted Amado; he was my beloved. He refused to speak to me.'

Jemma sat rocking slightly before she spoke again.

'So Jerry rescued me.'

She sighed dramatically, comically, inviting me into the kaleidoscope of her life.

I knew why her mother had called her Jemima Puddle Duck. Jemma needed to be wrapped in the feathery wings of someone who would love her.

I wanted to say that she was worth more but it seemed pointless.

Jemma turned away detached, absorbed, wrapped in stillness.

'Before I started at drama school, I was charring, mostly in Kensington because they paid better and gave you lunch. I was trying to find the address where they had advertised for a cleaner. I got the number wrong. The woman who answered the door smiled as though she knew me.'

'"My son died in the war twenty-seven years ago today". She looked past me up into the sky.

"I have loved him beyond eternity".

'Then she closed the door. It haunts me.'

'Why?'

Jemma took my hands and held them, all pretence gone.

'That is a secret.'

We lay together in her narrow bed in that awful, comfortless flat.

Jemma put her head on my shoulder.

'Go to sleep,' I said. 'I'll look after you.'

In the morning when we had finished our coffee, Jemma handed something to me.

I felt her reluctance even as I took the silver and brass bells; bound forever by her kindness and wisdom.

'Learn to be happy.'

London and the swinging sixties was full of people like us, living on the edge, seeking comfort from the tiny sound of the little bells.

Chapter Thirty-Three

I flew out of London into an endless afternoon that went on and on until I reached Toronto. There is so much water in Canada. Everywhere we flew, we went over lakes. The terminal was all concrete and glass and just about empty. I was met by my Uncle Joe. He and Aunt Emily were going to have to put up with me for about a month. I must have been crazy; it was almost three months before I eventually did get back. He stepped forward and kissed me. I shut my eyes when we got outside, not because of the glare but because of the tears in them.

Emily was already at the summer camp in Quebec. Joe had stayed back to meet me and we would be travelling up to the camp tomorrow. I went for a walk after Joe left me alone in the house, saying I probably wanted a nice quiet rest. It was no good telling him I had forgotten how to sleep, so I went for a walk instead. It was crushingly hot outside. I set off in the direction of the park he had told me about. The park was full of white concrete and smelled strange, of dead weed and chlorine. Somewhere, in that lost afternoon were red flowers. I can remember seeing them as everything else in me went to sleep far away from London.

It was fun travelling in an air-conditioned car, plush, even by American standards. The trip took all day. Joe asked me about my mother and father. I told him I had not managed to get back to Ireland since I had come to London. Not that I was afraid of my parents, I had phoned my father when I had arrived in London. My father had listened without speaking until I found the strength to hang up and walk out of the phone booth. I could not face Joe's polite disbelieving shock just then.

Emily was waiting up for us when we arrived at a large wooden log cabin in the middle of the trees we had been driving through. Emily looked elderly with the grey in her dark hair, her face tanned and pretty. She came forward and kissed me.

'Hi, Nina, it is good to see you again.'

She frowned, looking more closely at me.

'You need fattening up and a good sleep. Then you must tell me all about London. But for now, we are delighted to have you come and visit us.'

I wanted to say something but no words came. Joe went past us with my suitcase and then we all trooped into a main building. A huge log fire was burning in the grate. I sat down in front of it on a real white bearskin rug. Joe brought me a whisky on the rocks, which I sipped very carefully; we only went in for pot where I came from. The camp and the lake were completely isolated. Joe and Gordon, a college friend of Joe's who was a psychiatrist, used to come up here every summer to fish when they were students. Gordon had bought this camp with Joe. Now they and some of their friends spent part of their summers here. There were three other camps on the lake. The four camps were made of log cabins and had no electricity. No motor boats were allowed. They all had boathouses that you could not see because they were hidden away in the trees. Everyone had canoes, a sailboat and rowing boats for fishing.

I almost drowned in the same lake. I climbed up a tree that had a rope tied to one of its top branches. I took hold of the rope and swung out high over the water that closed over my head in a white, dark splash. I kicked up to the surface. I began to make for the diving platform that was nearer the middle of the lake than anywhere else. My arms and legs, everything, started to weigh a ton and I went down with them. The effort of staying afloat was too much. I went down again. When I came to the surface, I saw Gordon painting an old rowing boat. He glanced over to me. I knew I was not going to call for help. I could not cry out for help, not to save my life. I just let myself go on falling until I reached the bottom. It was the beginning of the rocks of the shoreline. I clawed my way along them, coming up to the surface to snatch desperately needed air until I came to where I could just stand. I made it to the shore with scratched hands and knees. I was trembling so much; I could not stand. I sat shivering, hugging my knees against me, looking out across the afternoon. I was cold sitting out on the rocks, so I got up and walked up the path that led to the boathouse. Gordon stopped me as I walked past.

'Are you alright?'

My throat closed over. I nodded. He put the paintbrush down.

'You must be careful.'

He indicated my scratched and bleeding hands.

'Why didn't you call for help?'

The boat had been painted bright red. It was still wet, the bright red paint. It smelled sharply of turpentine and I could see the soft wrinkle marks left by the fresh paint. They ran into each other in a bewildering mass of little lines that came and went. Then I couldn't hear anything.

The next day, Emily handed me a yellow pill. I asked her what the pill was for.

'Gordon thinks you need them.'

She kind of hovered over me while I took the pill.

'How are your parents? It seems awful but we only exchange letters once a year at Christmas. Your mother never writes, but Rupert does. I know your father is very proud of your academic achievements.'

Seeing my expression, she said,

'What's the matter, honey?'

When I did not reply, she went on as though speaking to herself.

'I did worry that the terrible accident could destroy their marriage and that would have been dreadful. Amy and Rupert always adored each other.'

The idea of my parents adoring each other seemed to comfort Emily. The truth of the matter was that their lives had been reduced to taunting each other through me; the spiteful destructive game they played was all that was left of the once carefree life they had enjoyed.

'Poor Amy,'

Emily sighed.

'She was always such fun.'

There were water lilies on the far side of the lake. Time had stopped here with days sliding into each other. I peeled some of the bark off one of the maple trees that came down to the edge of the lake in a shower of gold. Nothing was required of me. Here, I was able to withdraw into a silence of my making. The bark was soft and pliable; it felt like parchment. I wanted to write to Courtly and tell him about Canada and the camp and everything. I thought about it for a long time, looking out across the water. The lake held the reflection of the whole sky and the water lilies wax perfect as I touched the essence of the morning.

Chapter Thirty-Four

Toronto seemed to have died while I had been away. All it needed was a couple of newspapers floating around and it could have been the city in *On the Beach*.

While I was unpacking, Emily came into my room.

'Nina, Gordon thinks you are under a lot of pressure.'

Of course I was. I was trying to survive the swinging sixties as the Mother Superior.

'Gordon would like to see you in his rooms.'

'Why?' I was defensive.

Emily took my hand.

'Listen, honey, we are very worried about you. You are too thin and far too quiet. We spoke to Gordon. He is a psychiatrist. He would like to see you tomorrow and he thinks you should stay on.'

She put her arms around me.

'Don't feel bad about it, honey. I can imagine what you've been through. We're just glad to be able to help. That's all.'

She kissed me lightly on the top of my head and went out, relieved that Gordon was here to fix me. I felt weary beyond the saying of it. Sitting alone in that unfamiliar room, I felt as though I were inking in, in black, a picture of myself. That night for the first time in ages, I slept.

Gordon was sitting behind an executive desk. He did not get up when I came in or usher me to a chair.

'Hi, Nina, how are you?'

'Fine, but mad.'

Gordon laughed.

'Actually I think you remarkably sane.'

I wanted to ask then why I was there but anxiety stopped me.

I went to stand at the window away from him. Gordon watched me carefully before he spoke.

'Emily talked to me about your family situation, your parents' accident, your mother's attempted suicide and the permanent physical damage to your parents. There was no mention of you.'

I felt a sudden rush of anger.

'That was because I was invisible.'

Gordon leaned back in his chair away from me, cocking an eyebrow, a habit I was to associate with him.

'They didn't speak to me.'

I could say it because he didn't seem to take what I said seriously.

'Would you like to elaborate on that?'

It was as though I were telling someone else's story.

'After my mother came out of hospital, she stopped speaking.'

'Why was that?'

'She hated me?'

I wanted him to challenge me to explain away how I felt so it would not be true but he didn't.

'I didn't know what my mother looked like after the accident. I screamed when I saw her and she tried to kill herself because of me.'

'Don't you think your reaction might have been different if your father had warned you what to expect when you saw your mother again?'

I had been burdened for so long; I had nothing to say.

'By not telling you, your father was able to avoid some of his responsibility.'

He waited for me to speak and then went on.

'Did you believe if your mother died, it would have been all your fault?'

'Yes.'

I felt as though I were being emptied out. I was fearful if I did not escape him, I would break into pieces.

He got up from behind his desk.

'Why don't you sit down? This may take a while.'

It was a light-hearted invitation, giving me time to gather myself.

'Do you still believe that?'

I wanted to speak but I did not find any words.

Gordon stood thoughtfully watching me and then went on casually.

'Did your mother speak to your father?'

'No.'

'Did they communicate at all?'

'Yes.'

'How was that achieved?'

'My mother wrote notes that she put on the silver tray in the hall for me to take to my father. Her notes always made my father angry and he would shout sometimes, "Tell your mother…" But I could not speak to her, so I had to write down what my father said and leave the note for her.'

'Did they only communicate through you?'

'Yes.'

'How did that affect you?'

'Something went wrong in my head.'

'Can you explain that?'

'Often I can't think properly. Words get jumbled up in my head.'

'When did that start?'

'My father left two kittens in a basket as a surprise for my mother. Her cat had run away. She had called for him for days.'

'So your mother could speak?'

'Yes.'

I had not thought about that. I wanted to shrug that away from and me and my mother.

'She left a note to thank my father for kittens.'

'Your mother could have thanked your father personally.'

'I think she was afraid.'

'What was your mother afraid of?'

'We were all afraid.'

Gordon looked past me to the window at the bright sunny day outside, waiting for me to go on.

'I took the note my mother always left for me in the hall. My mother had drawn two hearts and written above them: Maxi and Millie.

I tore the message up and threw it away.'

'Do you know why you did that?'

'No, but afterwards, there were whisperers in my head, telling me of the harm I had done.'

'What harm had you done?'

'My father was so angry. He said, "Tell your mother that she would be more acceptable if she wore an eye patch. I have been punished enough". He hated my mother for not thanking him.'

I was in pain and hunched over.

'Would you like to stop?'

He was concerned, kind.

I shook my head, afraid if I did not say this now, I would never say it.

'Is that what you wrote?'

'Yes.'

'Did you give it to your mother?'

'I left the note in hall for her.'

'If you could pick out a word from the jumble in your head, what would it be?'

'I'm sorry.'

I said it without volition.

'Why?'

'If I had given my father my mother's note, they might have been happy again.'

'Is that what you wanted?'

I wanted to say yes.

'No.'

'Do you believe a note from your mother was all it took to redeem their toxic marriage?'

I didn't answer.

Gordon said quite casually.

'That's not your responsibility.'

I looked across at the lake, thousands of miles away from my mother and father who had so burdened me.

110

'I didn't ever take notes or speak again.'

'The silence must have been overwhelming?'

'Yes.'

'Is that what made you leave home?'

'My mother spoke to me.'

'What did you do?'

The words hung in the room, fearful echoes.

'I left home that day. I betrayed her.'

I remained huddled in the chair. I had nothing more to say.

The ornate clock on his desk chimed, my time was up.

On the street, a military band in bright red uniforms was playing a marching song of another country. I thought of Luca who waited for me every Thursday. He, like me, was guilty. We had both abandoned the people we loved.

Chapter Thirty-Five

Seeing a shrink was not an instant cure. I retreated to the basement to watch endless reruns of *Ben Casey* and living on a diet of peanut butter and jelly sandwiches. Gordon still prescribed little yellow pills that Emily dispensed, as sleep evaded me. Emily would drive me into Toronto to Gordon's rooms. To the maze of words, half-truths, fragmented memories and evasion as I spoke of London, the theatre and drama school in my distorted reasoning, the huge burden of an unasked for talent, an offer of success and the rejection I would not confront and my terrifying inertia. Gordon sat comfortably in his big armchair opposite me, listening without challenging what I said. I was waiting for him to ask the obligatory question, 'How do you feel about that?'

I would lie to him then because I didn't know the answer.

Gordon was back behind his desk. He reached for a cigar, indicating to me for permission.

Surprised, I laughed.

He waited for me to sit in the comfortable armchair. He didn't believe in couches.

'Why didn't you ever demand something for you?'

'I think my heart was frozen.'

'I believe that just might be the case.'

It was light-hearted, kind. Tears welled up. I dared not cry; I would dissolve into grief.

'I don't think that your parents understood the harm they were doing to you. Victimhood is often cruel. It justifies too much.'

Gordon leaned back behind his executive desk as though to make what he said less personal.

'You were a hostage as long as you accepted blame.'

I wanted to defend them, protect them. I was always sad when I thought about them.

'I wasn't a prisoner.'

'But you were home-schooled?'

'I used to go to the village.'

'Could you forget them?'

'No, I worried about them.'

'Why?'

I shook my head, confused.

'If you could talk to them now, what would you say to them?'

'It's not my fault.'

I was profoundly shocked that I said that.

'Is that why you were so compliant?'

'Yes.'

I hated saying that. It stifled me.

'Did you think it would absolve you?'

I sat for a long time, safe in Gordon's office, no longer alone with the jumbled thoughts and feelings that had held me prisoner when I had no words of my own.

He waited for me to answer.

'Yes.'

'Did you need to still think that?'

'No.'

'You know now that you were not responsible for any of the harmful content of the notes they gave you. That your parents created this situation to defer facing their reality.'

Gordon put his cigar carefully onto the ashtray on his desk, waiting for me to speak. When I did not, he remarked casually,

'Families can be troublesome.'

Smiling, he glanced at me for confirmation.

I looked out at the high-rise buildings of Toronto, the slanting sun catching the many empty windows. 'I can't imagine my mother and father without me,' I said forlornly.

'Without me, they are deaf and dumb.'

'Were you important to them?'

'They only had me.'

'What are you without them?'

The question sucked the breath out of me. I was aimless, unable to do anything, waiting for something that would free me.

'I sought forgiveness for my life.'

'Why?'

They were harmed and I was not.'

'How do you feel about that?'

That was the question that had been lying in wait for me. I had no need for deceit because I would not be judged.

'Helpless.'

'Is that why you agreed to be their messenger?'

He spoke lightly, making it easier for me to answer.

'I wanted to do something for them.'

'The go-between is always burdened and usually found guilty.'

He leaned forward with his elbows on his desk and said conspiratorially.

'Are you guilty?'

'No.'

I remembered out of nowhere, how I had longed to run away from the fear and sadness that stalked me. Somewhere, there were bright yellow daffodils. I was suddenly enchanted; there never had been anywhere to go.

Chapter Thirty-Six

Joe and Emily went up to Lake Muskoka where they had a small summer cottage that could only be reached by boat. Gordon was away, so my days were no longer regulated by my therapy sessions. Joe taught me to water ski. I loved skimming across the silky water of the lake. In the evenings, I toasted marshmallows on the open fireplace and learnt to play three-handed bridge. As the nights lengthened, I spoke of Jan, Pravin and Courtly, casting them on like stitches, weaving them into magical patterns as I talked myself into being. Except, Courtly was alive. I could only speak of him like that because I was afraid that he would be gone forever.

I stayed up reading Emily's old books, making sure I kept the fire going so that it would be warm in the morning when they woke up. I took a mug of freshly brewed coffee outside. Emily followed me onto the porch.

'Your father wrote that they will be leaving Ireland and returning to Kenya. He still has business interests there.'

Emily had been in touch with my parents to say that I was in Canada. She had also informed them that I was seeing a psychiatrist and being treated for chronic anxiety.

'I never understood why your parents chose to bury themselves in Ireland.'

'My father went away on business and my mother had her crosswords and her cats.'

'What did you have?'

'My parents.'

'I know what happened to Amy was awful but she must not let it ruin her life.'

But my mother's life was being beautiful. I could not explain that to Emily any more than I could comfort my mother.

'I spoke to Amy. Her main concern seems to be Millie and Maxi whoever they are?'

I laughed.

'Her cats, my father gave them to her when they were kittens.'

'Amy has been receiving treatment for her depression. Rupert has been very supportive. I hope Amy appreciates that. Rupert was always kind.'

'He was not kind to me.'

I said it without rancour.

'I know. I'm sorry.'

'Your father is very anxious now to do something for you. He has suggested that you might consider going to university in South Africa. He thinks a complete change would be beneficial.'

I was very surprised at how calm I felt.

'I am glad your parents are in touch again.'

'With you, not me.'

'It's a beginning.'

Emily gave me a quick hug. I put my hand against her cheek, brown and wrinkled, because she cared.

Summer had slipped away from me as I untangled the threads that had bound me so tightly.

It was our last weekend at Muskoka. Already boats were tied up under their awnings. Chill winds rippled across the water where the trees were reflected in red and gold.

My father, of the green ink, wrote to me. He told me about their planned return to Kenya and hoped that I would agree to study at university in South Africa. He was anxious that I get a formal education. His concern for me was expressed in the same terms as my private drama tutor. He wanted me to have a purpose that would afford me a safety net, that I would have a roof over my head. He had enclosed a gift, the trilogy of *The Lord of the Rings*.

Lying in the wrapping was a postcard with a picture of three cats. On one, my mother had drawn an eye patch and in a bubble she had written "Maxi, Millie and me". My funny beautiful mother. I was content as the lilies in the fields.

Chapter Thirty-Seven

I was meeting Gordon at the yacht club because he was officially still on holiday. The huge lake was quite different from the sea. It held you in, enclosed you. I walked along the quayside next to the boats that bobbed in the water. A woman walked towards me. She was tall and elegantly dressed in the uniform of boat owners, in white slacks and a tailored navy jacket. As we passed, she paused. Her dark hair pulled back from her face that was tanned and lined, lived in.

'You make a happy sound.'

My hands went up to the brass bells. She looked at me quizzically as though expecting me to say something.

I had only just begun to realise that I could decide the sound I made.

Then we walked past each other.

Gordon, casually dressed, was waiting for me at his reserved table.

'You are looking good.'

'How did you enjoy Muskoka?'

'I loved it.'

'Did Joe teach you to water ski?'

'Yes.'

He pushed out a chair for me to join him.

'Being happy agrees with you.'

I held something intangible close to me.

'My father has been in touch.'

Gordon looked at me appraisingly before he spoke.

'How?'

'He wrote to me. He wants me to go to university in South Africa.'

'Why South Africa?'

'They are planning to go back to Kenya. So we will be on the same continent.'

'What do you want to do?'

'My father believes a complete break would be beneficial, probably because my first move was such a failure.'

Gordon raised an eyebrow, disavowing what I had said.

'Is that what you think?'

I suddenly understood something very clearly.

'I didn't escape from them?'

'We can never escape our parents. Accountability and remorse can be extremely paralysing and you were unjustly burdened with both.'

'They are happy now that they are leaving Ireland.'

'Where does that leave you?'

He said it lightly.

I couldn't breathe. I was suddenly enraged. How dare they just get on with their lives when they had taken so much of mine?

'All this time I cared about them, but they didn't care about me.'

I thought that he had the missing pieces, that he would say something to comfort me. But Gordon was just listening. I knew the answer had to come from me.

I had wanted my parents to be judged and found guilty so I could blame them, but I already knew it was pointless. I turned away from everything that had happened; it was unimaginably simple.

The afternoon sun was spreading silver across the distant water, gathering the last of the day.

'I am going to miss Canada.'

'Then why don't you stay?'

The question was casual.

'No, I might begin to depend on you.'

There was a kindness and understanding in his smile.

'You are going to be just fine. So far, you have done all the right things to help yourself.'

My therapy was over.

Simple things like that were part of the key. I knew he accepted me and that he liked me. It's strange to have lost a step in the world and that all the days before were by-products of now. It matters because it will never happen again.

Then I remembered what my mother had said the day I left home.

'Long ago when we stayed at that funny old hotel with a long veranda.'

The words were awkward, misshapen from being so long withheld.

'There was a black rabbit. You were so excited when you saw the rabbit.'

I had not remembered, but my mother had.

'The rabbit came hopping up to you. You were very lonely and I was so delighted when rabbit came to visit you.'

Wild geese flew over. I watched until they were out of sight, the darkening red sky empty of their call, in the realisation now, that I had been loved.

Chapter Thirty-Eight

I wrote to Jan to tell him I was coming back, the flight number and time I would arrive, even though it was too early in the morning for him to meet me. I wrote it on the bark of a maple tree, putting a stamp on it to make it legal. Then I phoned my father. I had not spoken to him since I had left home. I could do this, not because of Gordon, or the pills. I could do this because of a teacher at drama school. He had told us of a courtesan living in Paris at the turn of the century. She was now old and ugly but still held court when most of her admirers had abandoned her. People thought of her as ridiculous, a pathetic figure. Daniel Benson delighted in her; because she was brave, she was magnificent. Gifts come from unexpected people.

My father's well-modulated familiar voice sounded hesitant, polite. I told him that I had decided to enrol for a BA in English, at Cape Town University in South Africa. We would be on same continent but I was no longer subject to them. The idea of rules and limits soothed me. I would learn someone else's words. Only this time, they would not hold me hostage.

'You need to be there by February. Your mother and I hope to see you before that. I thought we might fly down to Cape Town and get you settled in.'

'Thank you. I'd like that.'

Finally, I could do something for them.

'Your mother was happy in Kenya.'

'Yes, I remember.'

'I hope you find pleasure in your course; books have been my solace.'

They were allowing me to be free.

'I know your mother and I did a terrible thing, but that is no excuse to ruin the rest of your life.'

'No, I won't do that.'

'Look after yourself, my child.'

Then I wept for them and myself, something I had not done yet, the healing of the heart.

Emily planned a farewell dinner for me and took me shopping. Emily took my arm as we crossed the road. I really liked her. I would have been pretty sunk without them, but there they were when I needed them and it made me think. Perhaps there was a plan in things. I got a dress in the end, very simple, very elegant, dark Burgundy velvet.

'You look quite beautiful.'

I think Emily was glad to be able to be proud of me. After all, I was part of the family.

'I think Nina looks stunning,' Joe said proudly. I smiled and smiled like some idiot. I liked being part of the general hum of this. The dinner I had helped Emily prepare was lavish. She told me she wanted to put her best foot forward and when Gordon went into raptures about her cooking, she smiled and winked at me. They began to discuss what they would do during the winter months.

'What will you do?'

Emily asked.

'I'm not sure,' I said simply.

The future no longer held an impossible time I had to endure.

After dinner, Gordon gave me a gift.

It was a small beautiful jade Buddha.

'That's really something,' Emily said, a little awed.

'I know how superstitious you are. You can rub his tummy for luck.'

I weighed it in my hand.

'I got this on account of all those awful, depressing things I told you.'

'And this is part of the end product.'

I did not answer Gordon. I would have to think about that first.

Joe and Emily took me to the airport, staying with me until my flight was called.

'Come and visit us anytime,' Joe boomed.

'Thank you for everything.'

'And thank you for coming.'

Emily kissed me and I went through the glass partition to join the other passengers waiting at customs. Someone had dropped something, a small metal button, the ones you clip on and wear, with a slogan printed on it.

"Be a contributor".

I picked it up. I did not know what to do with it, so I kept it and without meaning to, I joined the human race.

Chapter Thirty-Nine

It was still dark when the plane landed. I caught the coach from the terminal looking out at the rows and rows of houses shut up under the orange street lights. I had not come back to London but myself.

Jan opened the front door. He was still half-asleep. His face changed when he looked at me.

'You're better.'

'Yes.'

I was glad that Jan knew and I could meet this with him, in the deserted street before it got light. We went into the kitchen. I sat on the stepladder holding Sometime, who had waited for us to come back. Jan made tea and we listened to *The Beatles* singing *Here Comes the Sun*.

The sun never shone. It would struggle against the cold milky white sky as the afternoon faded. The darkness from outside seeped into the house. Jan had managed to get a small part in the television drama while I was away. The BBC had used some of Robert's painting as set dressing. They gave Jan the part because he was there with Robert.

Now Jan was hoping that the agency he had signed up with would give him more work. It made him anxious and edgy, diminishing him. I was glad to be distracted by the official documents that had to be filled in and signed before I could leave. I wanted Jan to go back to the theatre where he would be safe, drinking tea with Stan. Robert, the beautiful, was becoming restless. Italy had confirmed he was destined for great things with the help of the ancient count he had come across during his "travels with my dick".

Robert was planning to return to Italy in the spring but he resisted chance encounters on the Putney Towpath, content to come back to Jan. Jan became more scattered and fearful as I signed the forms that would take me to Africa.

Pravin was back from his first term at Leeds University. He was in the kitchen with Sometime in his arms. There had been no one else to welcome him home.

Robert was leaning elegantly in the doorway.

So, when will you be contributing to the works of English literature?'

Pravin put Sometime carefully back on the stepladder, making sure he would not fall.

'I asked my English professor to read my novel.'

Robert shrugged dismissively.

'What was his opinion of the great opus one?'

'I thought someone would want to read what I wrote. My professor said it was not a book. It was just a collection of memories and that it showed no artistic merit.'

Robert laughed, 'At least you will be spared all the rejection slips.'

I said, 'Fuck you, Robert.'

Pravin looked blankly at Robert through his glasses. He made me think of Mole.

'I have to go to Scotland,' he was apologetic. 'My Auntie is dying.'

Pravin was helpless, alone in the kitchen. We were all he had and that was not saying much.

I gave Pravin the silver and brass bells. He needed them most, now he thought he could not write.

Jan and I went to the station to see Pravin off, buying him imported oranges and the *Evening Standard* to keep him company, along with the sound of the little bells. We waved to him as he went through the barriers. Pravin did not turn around because he always went to the station alone.

'I thought Pravin was going to make us immortal?'

Jan was looking back at the empty railway line.

'I don't want to be immortal.'

'No one ever remembers you,' Jan said forlornly.

'I'll remember you forever, I promise.'

We caught the bus from the station and were walking along The Embankment. It was very cold, with the sky burning red in the freezing end of the day. I would be going soon. I knew unbidden sadness and loneliness would come. I was afraid to stay. Jan would fly too close to the sun. He, like Icarus, had wings made of wax that would melt.

'I want to show you something.'

Big Ben began to chime. It was not really very late. It was just that it was winter; that's why it would soon be dark. We ran across the road away from the river.

'Look.'

On a street lamp cast in iron was a statue of two children, one passing a light to the other.

'I thought you would like to see it.'

'I didn't know it was there.'

'Do you like it?' he insisted.

'Yes,' I said, 'I do.'

Walking back, I took Jan's hand. It began to snow, wrapping London and us up for the night.

CPSIA information can be obtained
at www.ICGtesting.com
Printed in the USA
LVHW031302281122
734163LV00008B/371

9 781528 920292